£3.99

.2

.2 MAY 2004

WITHDRAWN

FROM

D1428934

WILLIAM TREVOR

Cocktails at Doney's & Other Stories

Selected by
Giles Gordon

BLOOMSBURY
CLASSICS

F/399775

Leabharla...l
Contae na Midhe

This selection published 1996
Copyright © William Trevor 1967, 1972, 1975, 1986, 1992,
1994
This selection © copyright Giles Gordon 1996

The moral right of the author has been asserted

Bloomsbury Publishing Plc,
2 Soho Square, London W1V 6HB

A CIP catalogue record for this book
is available from the British Library

ISBN 0 7475 2911 6

Jacket design by Jeff Fisher
Typeset in Great Britain by
Hewer Text Composition Services, Edinburgh
Printed in Great Britain

Acknowledgements

These stories were included in William Trevor's collections as follows: 'A Meeting in Middle Age' in *The Day We Got Drunk on Cake and Other Stories* (1967); 'The Ballroom of Romance' and 'The Grass Widows' in *The Ballroom of Romance and Other Stories* (1972); 'Broken Homes' and 'Death in Jerusalem' in *Angels at the Ritz and Other Stories* (1975); and 'Cocktails at Doney's' in *The News from Ireland and Other Stories* (1986). All these stories are included in William Trevor: *The Collected Stories* (Penguin, 1992). The publishers are grateful to Penguin Books for permission to reprint the stories here.

'Widows' was first published in *The New Yorker*, 27 June/4 July 1994 and is reprinted by permission of the author and Peters, Fraser & Dunlop.

CONTENTS

Cocktails at Doney's

'You've forgotten me,' were the first words Mrs Faraday spoke to him in the Albergo San Lorenzo. She was a tall, black-haired woman, wearing a rust-red suede coat cut in an Italian style. She smiled. She had white, even teeth, and the shade of her lipstick appeared subtly to match the colour of her coat. Her accent was American, her voice soft, with a trace of huskiness. She was thirty-five, perhaps thirty-seven, certainly not older. 'We met a long time ago,' she said, smiling a little more. 'I don't know why I never forget a face.'

She was married to a man who managed a business in some town in America he'd never heard of. She was a beautiful woman, but he could remember neither her nor her husband. Her name meant nothing to him and when she prompted him with the information about her husband's business he could not remember any better. Her eyes were brown, dominating her classic features.

'Of course,' he lied politely.

She laughed, clearly guessing it was a lie. 'Well, anyway,' she said, 'hullo to you.'

It was after dinner, almost ten o'clock. They had a drink in the bar since it seemed the natural thing to do. She had to do with fashion; she was in Florence for the Pitti Donna; she always came in February.

'It's nice to see you again. The people at these
trade shows can be tacky.'

'Don't you go to the museums as well? The
churches?'

'Of course.'

When he asked if her husband accompanied her
on her excursions to Florence she explained that the
museums, the churches, and the Pitti Donna would
tire her husband immensely. He was not a man for
Europe, preferring local race-tracks.

'And your wife? Is she here with you?'

'I'm actually not married.'

He wished he had not met Mrs Faraday. He didn't
care for being approached in this manner, and her
condemnation of the people at the trade exhibitions
she spoke of seemed out of place since they were,
after all, the people of her business world. And that
she was married to a man who preferred race-tracks
to culture was hardly of interest to a stranger. Before
their conversation ended he was certain they had not
ever met before.

'I have to say good-night,' he said, rising when she
finished her drink. 'I tend to get up early.'

'Why, so do I!'

'Good-night, Mrs Faraday.'

In his bedroom he sat on the edge of his bed,
thinking about nothing in particular. Then he
undressed and brushed his teeth. He examined his
face in the slightly tarnished looking-glass above the
wash-basin. He was fifty-seven, but according to
this reflection older. His face would seem younger
if he put on a bit of weight; chubbiness could be
made to cover a multitude of sins. But he didn't

want that; he liked being thought of as beyond things.

He turned the looking-glass light out and got into bed. He read *Our Mutual Friend* and then lay for a moment in the darkness. He thought of Daphne and of Lucy – dark-haired, tiny Lucy who had said at first it didn't matter, Daphne with her trusting eyes. He had blamed Daphne, not himself, and then had taken that back and asked to be forgiven; they were both of them to blame for the awful mistake of a marriage that should never have taken place, although later he had said that neither of them was, for how could they have guessed they were not suited in that way? It was with Lucy he had begun to know the truth; poor Lucy had suffered more.

He slept, and dreamed he was in Padua with a friend of another time, walking in the Botanical Gardens and explaining to his friend that the tourist guides he composed were short-lived in their usefulness because each reflected a city ephemerally caught. 'You're ashamed of your tourist guides,' his friend of that time interrupted, Jeremy it was. 'Why *are* the impotent so full of shame, my dear? Why *is* it?' Then Rosie was in the dream and Jeremy was laughing, playfully, saying he'd been most amusingly led up the garden path. 'He led me up it too, my God,' Rosie cried out furiously. 'All he could do was weep.'

Linger over the Giambologna birds in the Bargello, and the marble reliefs of Mino da Fiesole. But that's enough for one day; you must return tomorrow.

He liked to lay down the law. He liked to take chances with the facts, and wait for letters of contradiction. *At the height of the season there are twelve times as many strangers as natives in this dusty, littered city. Cascades of graffiti welcome them – the male sexual organ stylized to a Florentine simplicity, belligerent swastikas, hammers and sickles in the streets of gentle Fra Angelico . . .*

At lunchtime on the day after he had met her Mrs Faraday was in Doney's with some other Americans. Seeing her in that smart setting, he was surprised that she stayed in the Albergo San Lorenzo rather than the Savoy or the Excelsior. The San Lorenzo's grandeur all belonged to the past: the old hotel was threadbare now, its curtains creased, its telephones unresponsive. Not many Americans liked it.

'Hi!' she called across the restaurant, and smiled and waved a menu.

He nodded at her, not wishing to seem standoffish. The people she was with were talking about the merchandise they had been inspecting at the Pitti Donna. Wisps of their conversation drifted from their table, references to profit margins and catching the imagination.

He ordered tagliatelle and the chef's salad, and then looked through the *Nazione*. The body of the missing schoolgirl, Gabriella, had been found in a park in Florence. Youths who'd been terrorizing the neighbourhood of Santa Croce had been identified and arrested. Two German girls, hitchhiking in the south, had been made drunk and raped in a village shed. The *Nazione* suggested that Gabriella – a quiet girl – had by chance been a witness to drug-trafficking in the park.

'I envy you your job,' Mrs Faraday said, pausing at his table as he was finishing his tagliatelle. Her companions had gone on ahead of her. She smiled, as at an old friend, and then sat down. 'I guess I want to lose those two.'

He offered her a glass of wine. She shook her head. 'I'd love another cappuccino.'

The coffee was ordered. He folded the newspaper and placed it on the empty chair beside him. Mrs Faraday, as though she intended to stay a while, had hung her red suede coat over the back of the chair.

'I envy you your job,' she said again. 'I'd love to travel all over.'

She was wearing pearls at her throat, above a black dress. Rings clustered her fingers, earrings made a jangling sound. Her nails were shaped and painted, her face as meticulously made up as it had been the night before.

'Did you mind,' she asked when the waiter had brought their coffee, 'my wondering if you were married?'

He said he hadn't minded.

'Marriage is no great shakes.'

She lit a cigarette. She had only ever been married to the man she was married to now. She had had one child, a daughter who had died after a week. She had not been able to have other children.

'I'm sorry,' he said.

She looked at him closely, cigarette smoke curling between them. The tip of her tongue picked a shred of tobacco from the corner of her mouth. She said again that marriage was no great shakes. She added, as if to lend greater weight to this:

'I lay awake last night thinking I'd like this city to devour me.'

He did not comment, not knowing what she meant. But quite without wishing to he couldn't help thinking of this beautiful woman lying awake in her bedroom in the Albergo San Lorenzo. He imagined her staring into the darkness, the glow of her cigarette, the sound of her inhaling. She was looking for an affair, he supposed, and hoped she realized he wasn't the man for that.

'I wouldn't mind living the balance of my life here. I like it better every year.'

'Yes, it's a remarkable city.'

'There's a place called the Palazzo Ricasoli where you can hire apartments. I'd settle there.'

'I see.'

'I could tell you a secret about the Palazzo Ricasoli.'

'Mrs Faraday – '

'I spent a naughty week there once.'

He drank some coffee in order to avoid speaking. He sighed without making a sound.

'With a guy I met at the Pitti Donna. A countryman of yours. He came from somewhere called Horsham.'

'I've never been to Horsham.'

'Oh, my God, I'm embarrassing you!'

'No, not at all.'

'Gosh, I'm sorry! I really am! Please say it's all right.'

'I assure you, Mrs Faraday, I'm not easily shocked.'

'I'm an awful shady lady embarrassing a nice Englishman! Please say you forgive me.'

'There is absolutely nothing to forgive.'

'It was a flop, if you want to know.' She paused. 'Say, what do you plan to write in your guidebook about Florence?'

'Banalities mostly.'

'Oh, come *on*!'

He shrugged.

'I'll tell you a nicer kind of secret. You have the cleverest face I've seen in years!'

Still he did not respond. She stubbed her cigarette out and immediately lit another. She took a map out of her handbag and unfolded it. She said:

'Can you show me where Santo Spirito is?'

He pointed out the church and directed her to it, warning her against the motorists' signs which pursued a roundabout one-way route.

'You're very kind.' She smiled at him, lavishly exposing her dazzling, even teeth as if offering a reward for his help. 'You're a kind person,' she said. 'I can tell.'

He walked around the perimeter of the vast Cascine Park, past the fun-fair and the zoo and the race-track. It was pleasant in the February sunshine, the first green of spring colouring the twiggy hedges, birches delicate by the river. Lovers sprawled on the seats or in motor-cars, children carried balloons. Stalls sold meat and nuts, and Coca-Cola and 7-Up. Runners in training-suits jogged along the bicycle track. *Ho fame* a fat young man had scrawled on a piece of cardboard propped up in front of him, and slept while he waited for charity.

Rosie, when she'd been his friend, had said he wrote about Italian cities so that he could always be a stranger. Well, it was true, he thought in the Cascine Park, and in order to rid himself of a contemplation of his failed relationship with Rosie he allowed the beauty of Mrs Faraday again to invade his mind. Her beauty would have delighted him if her lipstick-stained cigarettes and her silly, repetitious chattering didn't endlessly disfigure it. Her husband was a good man, she had explained, but a good man was not always what a woman wanted. And it had come to seem all of a piece that her daughter had lived for only a week, and all of a piece also that no other children had been born, since her marriage was not worthy of children. It was the Annunciations in Santo Spirito she wanted to see, she had explained, because she loved Annunciations.

'Would it be wrong of me to invite you to dinner?' She rose from a sofa in the hall of the Albergo San Lorenzo as soon as she saw him, making no effort to disguise the fact that she'd been waiting for him. 'I'd really appreciate it if you'd accept.'

He wanted to reply that he would prefer to be left alone. He wanted to state firmly, once and for all, that he had never met her in the past, that she had no claims on him.

'You choose somewhere,' she commanded, with the arrogance of the beautiful.

In the restaurant she ate pasta without ceasing to talk, explaining to him that her boutique had been bought for her by her husband to keep her occupied and happy. It hadn't worked, she said, implying that although her fashion shop had kept her busy it hadn't brought her contentment. Her face, drained of all expression, was lovelier than he had so far seen it, so sad and fragile that it seemed not to belong to the voice that rattled on.

He looked away. The restaurant was decorated with modern paintings and was not completely full. A squat, elderly man sat on his own, conversing occasionally with waiters. A German couple spoke in whispers. Two men and a woman, talking rapidly in Italian, deplored the death of the schoolgirl, Gabriella.

'It must have been extraordinary for the Virgin Mary,' Mrs Faraday was saying. 'One moment she's reading a book and the next there's a figure with wings swooping in on her.' That only made sense, she suggested, when you thought of it as the Virgin's dream. The angel was not really there, the Virgin herself was not really reading in such plush surroundings. 'Later I guess she dreamed another angel came,' Mrs Faraday continued, 'to warn her of her death.'

He didn't listen. The waiter brought them grilled salmon and salad. Mrs Faraday lit a cigarette. She said:

'The guy I shacked up with in the Palazzo Ricasoli was no better than a gigolo. I guess I don't know why I did that.'

He did not reply. She stubbed her cigarette out, appearing at last to notice that food had been placed in front of her. She asked him about the painters of the Florentine Renaissance, and the city's aristocrats and patrons. She asked him why Savonarola had been burnt and he said Savonarola had made people feel afraid. She was silent for a moment, then leaned forward and put a hand on his arm.

'Tell me more about yourself. Please.'

Her voice, eagerly insistent, irritated him more than before. He told her superficial things, about the other Italian cities for which he'd written guide-books, about the hill towns of Tuscany, and the Cinque Terre. Because of his reticence she said when he ceased to speak:

'I don't entirely make you out.' She added that he was nicer to talk to than anyone she could think of. She might be drunk; it was impossible to say.

'My husband's never heard of the Medicis nor any stuff like this. He's never even heard of Masaccio, you appreciate that?'

'Yes, you've made it clear the kind of man your husband is.'

'I've ruined it, haven't I, telling you about the Palazzo Ricasoli?'

'Ruined what, Mrs Faraday?'

'Oh, I don't know.'

They sat for some time longer, finishing the wine and having coffee. Once she reached across the table and put her hand on one of his. She repeated what she had said before, that he was kind.

'It's late,' he said.

'I know, honey, I know. And you get up early.'

He paid the bill, although she protested that it was she who had invited him. She would insist on their having dinner together again so that she might have her turn. She took his arm on the street.

'Will you come with me to Maiano one day?'

'Maiano?'

'It isn't far. They say it's lovely to walk at Maiano.'

'I'm really rather occupied, you know.'

'Oh, God, I'm bothering you! I'm being a nuisance! Forget Maiano. I'm sorry.'

'I'm just trying to say, Mrs Faraday, that I don't think I can be much use to you.'

He was aware, to his embarrassment, that she was holding his hand. Her arm was entwined with his and the palms of their hands had somehow come together. Her fingers, playing with his now, kept time with her flattery.

'You've got the politest voice I ever heard! Say you'll meet me just once again? Just once? Cocktails tomorrow? Please.'

'Look, Mrs Faraday – '

'Say Doney's at six. I'll promise to say nothing if you like. We'll listen to the music.'

Her palm was cool. A finger made a circular motion on one of his. Rosie had said he limped through life. In the end Jeremy had been sorry for him. Both of them were right; others had said worse. He was a crippled object of pity.

'Well, all right.'

She thanked him in the Albergo San Lorenzo for listening to her, and for the dinner and the wine. 'Every year I hope to meet someone nice in Florence,' she said on the landing outside her bedroom, seeming to mean it. 'This is the first time it has happened.'

She leaned forward and kissed him on the cheek, then closed her door. In his looking-glass he examined the faint smear of lipstick and didn't wipe it off. He woke in the night and lay there

thinking about her, wondering if her lipstick was
still on his cheek.

Waiting in Doney's, he ordered a glass of chilled
Orvieto wine. Someone on a tape, not Judy Garland,
sang 'Over the Rainbow'; later there was lightly
played Strauss and some rhythms of the thirties. By
seven o'clock Mrs Farady had not arrived. He left at a
quarter to eight.

The next day he wandered through the cloisters of
Santa Maria Novella, thinking again about the beauty
of Mrs Faraday. He had received no message from
her, no note to explain or apologize for her absence
in Doney's. Had she simply forgotten? Or had
someone better materialized? Some younger man
she again hadn't been able to resist, some guy who
didn't know any more about Masaccio than her good
husband did? She was a woman who was always
falling in love, which was what she called it, confus-
ing love with sensuality. Was she, he wondered, what
people referred to as a nymphomaniac? Was that
what made her unhappy?

    He imagined her with some man she'd picked up.
He imagined her, satisfied because of the man's
attentions, tramping the halls of a gift market, noting
which shade of green was to be the new season's
excitement. She would be different after her love-
making, preoccupied with her business, no time for
silliness and Annunciations. Yet it still was odd that
she hadn't left a message for him. She had not for a
moment seemed as rude as that, or incapable of
making up an excuse.

He left the cloisters and walked slowly across the piazza of Santa Maria Novella. In spite of what she'd said and the compliments she'd paid, had she guessed that he hadn't listened properly to her, that he'd been fascinated by her appearance but not by her? Or had she simply guessed the truth about him?

That evening she was not in the bar of the hotel. He looked in at Doney's, thinking he might have misunderstood about the day. He waited for a while, and then ate alone in the restaurant with the modern paintings.

'We pack the clothes, *signore*. Is the carabinieri which can promote the inquiries for *la signora*. *Mi dispiace, signore.*'

He nodded at the heavily moustached receptionist and made his way to the bar. If she was with some lover she would have surfaced again by now: it was hard to believe that she would so messily leave a hotel bill unpaid, especially since sooner or later she would have to return for her clothes. When she had so dramatically spoken of wishing Florence to devour her she surely hadn't meant something like this? He went back to the receptionist.

'Did Mrs Faraday have her passport?'

'*Sì, signore. La signora* have the passport.'

He couldn't sleep that night. Her smile and her brown, languorous eyes invaded the blur he attempted to induce. She crossed and re-crossed her legs. She lifted another glass. Her ringed fingers stubbed another cigarette. Her earrings lightly jangled.

In the morning he asked again at the reception desk. The hotel bill wasn't important, a different receptionist generously allowed. If someone had to leave Italy in a hurry, because maybe there was sickness, even a deathbed, then a hotel bill might be overlooked for just a little while.

'*La signora* will post to us a cheque from the United States. This the carabinieri say.'

'Yes, I should imagine so.'

He looked up in the telephone directory the flats she had mentioned. The Palazzo Ricasoli was in Via Mantellate. He walked to it, up Borgo San Lorenzo and Via San Gallo. '*No*,' a porter in a glass kiosk said and directed him to the office. '*No*,' a pretty girl in the office said, shaking her head. She turned and asked another girl. '*No*,' this girl repeated.

He walked back through the city, to the American Consulate on the Lungarno Amerigo. He sat in the office of a tall, lean man called Humber, who listened with a detached air and then telephoned the police. After nearly twenty minutes he replaced the receiver. He was dressed entirely in brown – suit, shirt, tie, shoes, handkerchief. He was evenly tanned, another shade of the colour. He drawled when he spoke; he had an old-world manner.

'They suggest she's gone somewhere,' he said. 'On some kind of jaunt.' He paused in order to allow a flicker of amusement to develop in his lean features. 'They think maybe she ran up her hotel bill and skipped it.'

'She's a respectable proprietor of a fashion shop.'

'The carabinieri say the respectable are always surprising them.'

'Can you try to find out if she went back to the States? According to the hotel people, that was another theory of the carabinieri.'

Mr Humber shrugged. 'Since you have told your tale I must try, of course, sir. Would six-thirty be an agreeable hour for you to return?'

He sat outside in the Piazza della Repubblica, eating tortellini and listening to the conversations. A deranged man had gone berserk in a school in Rome, taking children as hostages and killing a janitor; the mayor of Rome had intervened and the madman had given himself up. It was a terrible thing to have happened, the Italians were saying, as bad as the murder of Gabriella.

He paid for his tortellini and went away. He climbed up to the Belvedere, filling in time. Once he thought he saw her, but it was someone else in the same kind of red coat.

'She's not back home,' Mr Humber said with his old-world lack of concern. 'You've started something, sir. Faraday's flying out.'

In a room in a police station he explained that Mrs Faraday had simply been a fellow-guest at the Albergo San Lorenzo. They had had dinner one evening, and Mrs Faraday had not appeared to be dispirited. She knew other people who had come from America, for the same trade exhibitions. He had seen her with them in a restaurant.

'These people, sir, return already to the United States. They answer the American police at this time.'

He was five hours in the room at the police station and the next day he was summoned there again and asked the same questions. On his way out on this occasion he noticed a man who he thought might be her husband, a big blond-haired man, too worried even to glance at him. He was certain he had never met him, or even seen him before, as he'd been certain he'd never met Mrs Faraday before she'd come up to him in the hotel.

The police did not again seek to question him. His passport, which they had held for fifty-six hours, was returned to him. By the end of that week the newspaper references to a missing American woman ceased. He did not see Mr Faraday again.

'The Italian view,' said Mr Humber almost a month later, 'is that she went off on a sexual excursion and found it so much to her liking that she stayed where she was.'

'I thought the Italian view was that she skipped the hotel. Or that someone had fallen ill.'

'They revised their thinking somewhat. In the light of various matters.'

'What matters?'

'From what you said, Mrs Faraday was a gallivanting lady. Our Italian friends find some significance in that.' Mr Humber silently drummed the surface of his desk. 'You don't agree, sir?'

He shook his head. 'There was more to Mrs Faraday than that,' he said.

'Well, of course there was. The carabinieri are educated men, but they don't go in for subtleties, you know.'

'She's not a vulgar woman. From what I said to the police they may imagine she is. Of course she's in a vulgar business. They may have jumped too easily to conclusions.'

Mr Humber said he did not understand. 'Vulgar?' he repeated.

'Like me, she deals in surface dross.'

'You're into fashion yourself, sir?'

'No, I'm not. I write tourist guides.'

'Well, that's most interesting.'

Mr Humber flicked at the surface of his desk with a forefinger. It was clear that he wished his visitor would go. He turned a sheet of paper over.

'I remind sightseers that pictures like Pietro Perugino's *Agony in the Garden* are worth a second glance. I send them to the Boboli Gardens. That kind of thing.'

Mr Humber's bland face twitched with simulated interest. Tourists were a nuisance to him. They lost their passports, they locked their ignition keys into their hired cars, they were stolen from and made a fuss. The city lived off them, but resented them as well. These thoughts were for a moment openly reflected in Mr Humber's pale brown eyes and then were gone. Flicking at his desk again, he said:

'I'm puzzled about one detail in all this. May I ask you, please?'

'Yes, of course.'

'Were you, you know, ah, seeing Mrs Faraday?'

'Was I having an affair, you mean? No, I wasn't.'

'She was a beautiful woman. By all accounts – by yours, I mean – sir, she'd been most friendly.'

'Yes, she was friendly.'

She was naïve for an American, and she was careless. She wasn't fearful of strangers and foolishly she let her riches show. Vulnerability was an enticement.

'I did not mean to pry, sir,' Mr Humber apologized. 'It's simply that Mr Faraday's detectives arrived a while ago and the more they can be told the better.'

'They haven't approached me.'

'No doubt they conclude you cannot help them. Mr Faraday himself has returned to the States: a ransom note would be more likely sent to him there.'

'So Mr Faraday doesn't believe his wife went off on a sexual excursion?'

'No one can ignore the facts, sir. There is indiscriminate kidnapping in Italy.'

'Italians would have known her husband was well-to-do?'

'I guess it's surprising what can be ferreted out.' Mr Humber examined the neat tips of his fingers. He rearranged tranquillity in his face. No matter how the facts he spoke of changed there was not going to be panic in the American Consulate. 'There has been no demand, sir, but we have to bear in mind that kidnap attempts do often nowadays go wrong. In Italy as elsewhere.'

'Does Mr Faraday think it has gone wrong?'

'Faraday is naturally confused. And, of course, troubled.'

'Of course.' He nodded to emphasize his agreement. Her husband was the kind who would be troubled and confused, even though unhappiness had developed in the marriage. Clearly she'd given up on the marriage; more than anything, it was desperation that made her forthright. Without it, she might have been a different woman – and in that case, of course, there would not have been this passing relationship

between them: her tiresomeness had cultivated that.
'Tell me more about yourself,' her voice echoed
huskily, hungry for friendship. He had told her
nothing – nothing of the shattered, destroyed rela-
tionships, and the regret and shame; nothing of the
pathetic hope in hired rooms, or the anguish turning
into bitterness. She had been given beauty, and he a
lameness that people laughed at when they knew.
Would her tiresomeness have dropped from her at
once, like the shedding of a garment she had thought
to be attractive, if he'd told her in the restaurant with
the modern paintings? Would she, too, have angrily
said he'd led her up the garden path?

'There is our own investigation also,' Mr Humber
said, 'besides that of Faraday's detectives. Faraday, I
assure you, has spared no expense; the carabinieri file
is by no means closed. With such a concentration
we'll find what there is to find, sir.'

'I'm sure you'll do your best, Mr Humber.'

'Yes, *sir*.'

He rose and Mr Humber rose also, holding out a
brown, lean hand. He was glad they had met,
Mr Humber said, even in such unhappy circumstances. Diplomacy was like oil in Mr Humber. It
eased his movements and his words; his detachment
floated in it, perfectly in place.

'Goodbye, Mr Humber.'

Ignoring the lift, he walked down the stairs of the
Consulate. He knew that she was dead. He imagined
her lying naked in a wood, her even teeth ugly in a
rictus, her white flesh as lifeless as the virgin modesty
of the schoolgirl in the park. She hadn't been like a
nymphomaniac, or even a sophisticated woman,

when she'd kissed his cheek good-night. Like a
schoolgirl herself, she'd still been blind to the icy
coldness that answered her naïveté. Inept and academic, words he had written about the city which
had claimed her slipped through his mind. *In the
church of Santa Croce you walk on tombs, searching for
Giotto's Life of St Francis. In Savonarola's own piazza
the grey stone features do not forgive the tumbling hair of
pretty police girls or the tourists' easy ways.* Injustice and
harsh ambition had made her city what it was, the
violence of greed for centuries had been its blood-
stream; beneath its tinsel skin there was an iron heart.
*The Florentines, like true provincials, put work and money
first. In the Piazza Signoria the pigeons breakfast off the
excrement of the hackney horses: in Florence nothing is
wasted.*

He left the American Consulate and slowly walked
along the quay. The sun was hot, the traffic noisy. He
crossed the street and looked down into the green
water of the Arno, wondering if the dark shroud of
Mrs Faraday's life had floated away through a night.
In the galleries of the Uffizi he would move from
Annunciation to Annunciation, Simone Martini's,
Baldovinetti's, Lorenzo di Credi's, and all the
others. He would catch a glimpse of her red coat
in Santa Trinità, but the face would again be someone else's. She would call out from a *gelateria*, but the
voice would be an echo in his memory.

He turned away from the river and at the same
slow pace walked into the heart of the city. He sat
outside a café in the Piazza della Repubblica,
imagining her thoughts as she had lain in bed on
that last night, smoking her cigarettes in the darkness.

She had arrived at the happiest moment of love, when nothing was yet destroyed, when anticipation was a richness in itself. She'd thought about their walk in Maiano, how she'd bring the subject up again, how this time he'd say he'd be delighted. She'd thought about their being together in an apartment in the Palazzo Ricasoli, how this time it would be different. Already she had made up her mind: she would not ever return to the town where her husband managed a business. 'I have never loved anyone like this,' she whispered in the darkness.

In his hotel bedroom he shaved and had a bath and put on a suit that had just been pressed. In a way that had become a ceremony for him since the evening he had first waited for her there, he went at six o'clock to Doney's. He watched the Americans drinking cocktails, knowing it was safe to be there because she would not suddenly arrive. He listened to the music she'd said she liked, and mourned her as a lover might.

The Ballroom of Romance

On Sundays, or on Mondays if he couldn't make it and often he couldn't, Sunday being his busy day, Canon O'Connell arrived at the farm in order to hold a private service with Bridie's father, who couldn't get about any more, having had a leg amputated after gangrene had set in. They'd had a pony and cart then and Bridie's mother had been alive: it hadn't been difficult for the two of them to help her father on to the cart in order to make the journey to Mass. But two years later the pony had gone lame and eventually had to be destroyed; not long after that her mother had died. 'Don't worry about it at all,' Canon O'Connell had said, referring to the difficulty of transporting her father to Mass. 'I'll slip up by the week, Bridie.'

The milk lorry called daily for the single churn of milk, Mr Driscoll delivered groceries and meal in his van, and took away the eggs that Bridie had collected during the week. Since Canon O'Connell had made his offer, in 1953, Bridie's father hadn't left the farm.

As well as Mass on Sundays and her weekly visits to a wayside dance-hall Bridie went shopping once every month, cycling to the town early on a Friday afternoon. She bought things for herself, material for a dress, knitting wool, stockings, a newspaper, and paper-backed Wild West novels for her father. She talked in the shops to some of the girls she'd been at school with, girls who had married shop-assistants or shopkeepers, or had become assistants themselves. Most of them had families of their own by now. 'You're lucky to be peaceful in the hills,' they said to Bridie, 'instead of stuck in a hole like this.' They had a tired look, most of them, from pregnancies and their efforts to organize and control their large families.

As she cycled back to the hills on a Friday Bridie often felt that they truly envied her life, and she found it surprising that they should do so. If it hadn't been for her father she'd have wanted to work in the town also, in the tinned-meat factory maybe, or in a shop. The town had a cinema called the Electric, and a fish-and-chip shop where people met at night, eating chips out of newspaper on the pavement outside. In the evenings, sitting in the farmhouse with her father, she often thought about the town, imagining the shop-windows lit up to display their goods and the sweet-shops still open so that people could purchase chocolates or fruit to take with them to the Electric cinema. But the town was eleven miles away, which was too far to cycle, there and back, for an evening's entertainment.

'It's a terrible thing for you, girl,' her father used to say, genuinely troubled, 'tied up to a one-legged man.' He would sigh heavily, hobbling back from the fields, where he managed as best he could. 'If your mother hadn't died,' he'd say, not finishing the sentence.

If her mother hadn't died her mother could have looked after him and the scant acres he owned, her mother could somehow have lifted the milk-churn

on to the collection platform and attended to the few
hens and the cows. 'I'd be dead without the girl to
assist me,' she'd heard her father saying to Canon
O'Connell, and Canon O'Connell replied that he
was certainly lucky to have her.

'Amn't I as happy here as anywhere?' she'd say
herself, but her father knew she was pretending and
was saddened because the weight of circumstances
had so harshly interfered with her life.

Although her father still called her a girl, Bridie
was thirty-six. She was tall and strong: the skin of
her fingers and her palms were stained, and harsh
to touch. The labour they'd experienced had
found its way into them, as though juices had
come out of vegetation and pigment out of soil:
since childhood she'd torn away the rough scotch
grass that grew each spring among her father's
mangolds and sugar beet; since childhood she'd
harvested potatoes in August, her hands daily
rooting in the ground she loosened and turned.
Wind had toughened the flesh of her face, sun had
browned it; her neck and nose were lean, her lips
touched with early wrinkles.

But on Saturday nights Bridie forgot the scotch
grass and the soil. In different dresses she cycled to
the dance-hall, encouraged to make the journey by
her father. 'Doesn't it do you good, girl?' he'd say, as
though he imagined she begrudged herself the
pleasure. 'Why wouldn't you enjoy yourself?' She'd
cook him his tea and then he'd settle down with the
wireless, or maybe a Wild West novel. In time, while
still she danced, he'd stoke the fire up and hobble his
way upstairs to bed.

The dance-hall, owned by Mr Justin Dwyer, was miles from anywhere, a lone building by the roadside with treeless boglands all around and a gravel expanse in front of it. On pink pebbled cement its title was painted in an azure blue that matched the depth of the background shade yet stood out well, unfussily proclaiming *The Ballroom of Romance*. Above these letters four coloured bulbs – in red, green, orange and mauve – were lit at appropriate times, an indication that the evening rendezvous was open for business. Only the façade of the building was pink, the other walls being a more ordinary grey. And inside, except for pink swing-doors, everything was blue.

On Saturday nights Mr Justin Dwyer, a small, thin man, unlocked the metal grid that protected his property and drew it back, creating an open mouth from which music would later pour. He helped his wife to carry crates of lemonade and packets of biscuits from their car, and then took up a position in the tiny vestibule between the drawn-back grid and the pink swing-doors. He sat at a card-table, with money and tickets spread out before him. He'd made a fortune, people said: he owned other ballrooms also.

People came on bicycles or in old motor-cars, country people like Bridie from remote hill farms and villages. People who did not often see other people met there, girls and boys, men and women. They paid Mr Dwyer and passed into his dance-hall, where shadows were cast on pale-blue walls and light from a crystal bowl was dim. The band, known as the Romantic Jazz Band, was composed

of clarinet, drums and piano. The drummer sometimes sang.

Bridie had been going to the dance-hall since first
she left the Presentation Nuns, before her mother's
death. She didn't mind the journey, which was seven
miles there and seven back: she'd travelled as far
every day to the Presentation Nuns on the same
bicycle, which had once been the property of her
mother, an old Rudge purchased originally in 1936.
On Sundays she cycled six miles to Mass, but she
never minded either: she'd grown quite used to all
that.

'How're you, Bridie?' inquired Mr Justin Dwyer
when she arrived in a new scarlet dress one autumn
evening. She said she was all right and in reply to
Mr Dwyer's second query she said that her father was
all right also. 'I'll go up one of these days,' promised
Mr Dwyer, which was a promise he'd been making
for twenty years.

She paid the entrance fee and passed through the
pink swing-doors. The Romantic Jazz Band was
playing a familiar melody of the past, 'The Destiny
Waltz'. In spite of the band's title, jazz was not ever
played in the ballroom: Mr Dwyer did not personally
care for that kind of music, nor had he cared for
various dance movements that had come and gone
over the years. Jiving, rock and roll, twisting and
other such variations had all been resisted by
Mr Dwyer, who believed that a ballroom should
be, as much as possible, a dignified place. The
Romantic Jazz Band consisted of Mr Maloney,
Mr Swanton, and Dano Ryan on drums. They were
three middle-aged men who drove out from the town

in Mr Maloney's car, amateur performers who were employed otherwise by the tinned-meat factory, the Electricity Supply Board and the County Council.

'How're you, Bridie?' inquired Dano Ryan as she passed him on her way to the cloakroom. He was idle for a moment with his drums, 'The Destiny Waltz' not calling for much attention from him.

'I'm all right, Dano,' she said. 'Are you fit yourself? Are the eyes better?' The week before he'd told her that he'd developed a watering of the eyes that must have been some kind of cold or other. He'd woken up with it in the morning and it had persisted until the afternoon: it was a new experience, he'd told her, adding that he'd never had a day's illness or discomfort in his life.

'I think I need glasses,' he said now, and as she passed into the cloakroom she imagined him in glasses, repairing the roads, as he was employed to do by the County Council. You hardly ever saw a road-mender with glasses, she reflected, and she wondered if all the dust that was inherent in his work had perhaps affected his eyes.

'How're you, Bridie?' a girl called Eenie Mackie said in the cloakroom, a girl who'd left the Presentation Nuns only a year ago.

'That's a lovely dress, Eenie,' Bridie said. 'Is it nylon, that?'

'Tricel actually. Drip-dry.'

Bridie took off her coat and hung it on a hook. There was a small wash-basin in the cloakroom above which hung a discoloured oval mirror. Used tissues and pieces of cotton-wool, cigarette-butts and matches covered the concrete floor. Lengths of green-painted timber partitioned off a lavatory in a corner.

'Jeez, you're looking great, Bridie,' Madge Dowding remarked, waiting for her turn at the mirror. She moved towards it as she spoke, taking off a pair of spectacles before endeavouring to apply make-up to the lashes of her eye. She stared myopically into the oval mirror, humming while the other girls became restive.

'Will you hurry up, for God's sake!' shouted Eenie Mackie. 'We're standing here all night, Madge.'

Madge Dowding was the only one who was older than Bridie. She was thirty-nine, although often she said she was younger. The girls sniggered about that, saying that Madge Dowding should accept her condition – her age and her squint and her poor complexion – and not make herself ridiculous going out after men. What man would be bothered with the like of her anyway? Madge Dowding would do better to give herself over to do Saturday-night work for the Legion of Mary: wasn't Canon O'Connell always looking for aid?

'Is that fellow there?' she asked now, moving away from the mirror. 'The guy with the long arms. Did anyone see him outside?'

'He's dancing with Cat Bolger,' one of the girls replied. 'She has herself glued to him.'

'Lover boy,' remarked Patty Byrne, and everyone laughed because the person referred to was hardly a boy any more, being over fifty it was said, a bachelor who came only occasionally to the dance-hall.

Madge Dowding left the cloakroom rapidly, not bothering to pretend she wasn't anxious about the conjunction of Cat Bolger and the man with the long arms. Two sharp spots of red had come into her cheeks, and when she stumbled in her haste the girls in the cloakroom laughed. A younger girl would have pretended to be casual.

Bridie chatted, waiting for the mirror. Some girls, not wishing to be delayed, used the mirrors of their compacts. Then in twos and threes, occasionally singly, they left the cloakroom and took their places on upright wooden chairs at one end of the dance-hall, waiting to be asked to dance. Mr Maloney, Mr Swanton and Dano Ryan played 'Harvest Moon' and 'I Wonder Who's Kissing Her Now' and 'I'll Be Around'.

Bridie danced. Her father would be falling asleep by the fire; the wireless, tuned in to Radio Eireann, would be murmuring in the background. Already he'd have listened to *Faith and Order* and *Spot the Talent*. His Wild West novel, *Three Rode Fast* by Jake Matall, would have dropped from his single knee on to the flagged floor. He would wake with a jerk as he did every night and, forgetting what night it was, might be surprised not to see her, for usually she was sitting there at the table, mending clothes or washing eggs. 'Is it time for the news?' he'd automatically say.

Dust and cigarette smoke formed a haze beneath the crystal bowl, feet thudded, girls shrieked and laughed, some of them dancing together for want of a male partner. The music was loud, the musicians had taken off their jackets. Vigorously they played a number of tunes from *State Fair* and then, more romantically, 'Just One of Those Things'. The tempo increased for a Paul Jones, after which Bridie found herself with a youth who told her he was saving up to emigrate, the nation in his opinion being finished. 'I'm up in the hills with the uncle,' he said, 'labouring fourteen hours a day. Is it any life for a young fellow?' She knew his uncle, a hill farmer whose stony acres were separated from her father's by one other farm only. 'He has me gutted with work,' the youth told her. 'Is there sense in it at all, Bridie?'

At ten o'clock there was a stir, occasioned by the arrival of three middle-aged bachelors who'd cycled over from Carey's public house. They shouted and whistled, greeting other people across the dancing area. They smelt of stout and sweat and whiskey.

Every Saturday at just this time they arrived, and, having sold them their tickers, Mr Dwyer folded up his card-table and locked the tin box that held the evening's takings: his ballroom was complete.

'How're you, Bridie?' one of the bachelors, known as Bowser Egan, inquired. Another one, Tim Daly, asked Patty Byrne how she was. 'Will we take the floor?' Eyes Horgan suggested to Madge Dowding, already pressing the front of his navy-blue suit against the net of her dress. Bridie danced with Bowser Egan, who said she was looking great.

The bachelors would never marry, the girls of the dance-hall considered: they were wedded already, to stout and whiskey and laziness, to three old mothers somewhere up in the hills. The man with the long arms didn't drink but he was the same in all other ways: he had the same look of a bachelor, a quality in his face.

'Great,' Bowser Egan said, feather-stepping in an inaccurate and inebriated manner. 'You're a great little dancer, Bridie.'

'Will you lay off that!' cried Madge Dowding, her voice shrill above the sound of the music. Eyes Horgan had slipped two fingers into the back of her dress and was now pretending they'd got there by accident. He smiled blearily, his huge red face streaming with perspiration, the eyes which gave him his nickname protuberant and bloodshot.

'Watch your step with that one,' Bowser Egan called out, laughing so that spittle sprayed on to Bridie's face. Eenie Mackie, who was also dancing near the incident, laughed also and winked at Bridie. Dano Ryan left his drums and sang. 'Oh, how I miss your gentle kiss,' he crooned, 'and long to hold you tight.'

Nobody knew the name of the man with the long arms. The only words he'd ever been known to speak in the Ballroom of Romance were the words that formed his invitation to dance. He was a shy man who stood alone when he wasn't performing on the dance-floor. He rode away on his bicycle afterwards, not saying good-night to anyone.

'Cat has your man leppin' tonight,' Tim Daly remarked to Patty Byrne, for the liveliness that Cat Bolger had introduced into foxtrot and waltz was noticeable.

'I think of you only,' sang Dano Ryan. 'Only wishing, wishing you were by my side.'

Dano Ryan would have done, Bridie often thought, because he was a different kind of bachelor: he had a lonely look about him, as if he'd

become tired of being on his own. Every week she
thought he would have done, and during the week
her mind regularly returned to that thought. Dano
Ryan would have done because she felt he wouldn't
mind coming to live in the farmhouse while her one-
legged father was still about the place. Three could
live as cheaply as two where Dano Ryan was
concerned because giving up the wages he earned
as a road-worker would be balanced by the saving
made on what he paid for lodgings. Once, at the end
of an evening, she'd pretended that there was a
puncture in the back wheel of her bicycle and he'd
concerned himself with it while Mr Maloney and
Mr Swanton waited for him in Mr Maloney's car.
He'd blown the tyre up with the car pump and had
said he thought it would hold.

It was well known in the dance-hall that she
fancied her chances with Dano Ryan. But it was
well known also that Dano Ryan had got into a set
way of life and had remained in it for quite some
years. He lodged with a widow called Mrs Griffin
and Mrs Griffin's mentally affected son, in a cottage
on the outskirts of the town. He was said to be good
to the affected child, buying him sweets and taking
him out for rides on the crossbar of his bicycle. He
gave an hour or two of his time every week to the
Church of Our Lady Queen of Heaven, and he was
loyal to Mr Dwyer. He performed in the two other
rural dance-halls that Mr Dwyer owned, rejecting
advances from the town's more sophisticated dance-
hall, even though it was more conveniently situated
for him and the fee was more substantial than that
paid by Mr Dwyer. But Mr Dwyer had discovered

Dano Ryan and Dano had not forgotten it, just as Mr Maloney and Mr Swanton had not forgotten their discovery by Mr Dwyer either.

'Would we take a lemonade?' Bowser Egan suggested. 'And a packet of biscuits, Bridie?'

No alcoholic liquor was ever served in the Ballroom of Romance, the premises not being licensed for this added stimulant. Mr Dwyer in fact had never sought a licence for any of his premises, knowing that romance and alcohol were difficult commodities to mix, especially in a dignified ballroom. Behind where the girls sat on the wooden chairs Mr Dwyer's wife, a small stout woman, served the bottles of lemonade, with straws, and the biscuits, and crisps. She talked busily while doing so, mainly about the turkeys she kept. She'd once told Bridie that she thought of them as children.

'Thanks,' Bridie said, and Bowser Egan led her to the trestle table. Soon it would be the intermission: soon the three members of the band would cross the floor also for refreshment. She thought up questions to ask Dano Ryan.

When first she'd danced in the Ballroom of Romance, when she was just sixteen, Dano Ryan had been there also, four years older than she was, playing the drums for Mr Maloney as he played them now. She'd hardly noticed him then because of his not being one of the dancers: he was part of the ballroom's scenery, like the trestle table and the lemonade bottles, and Mrs Dwyer and Mr Dwyer. The youths who'd danced with her then in their Saturday-night blue suits had later disappeared into the town, or to Dublin or Britain, leaving behind them those who became the middle-aged bachelors of the hills. There'd been a boy called Patrick Grady whom she had loved in those days. Week after week she'd ridden away from the Ballroom of Romance with the image of his face in her mind, a thin face, pale beneath black hair. It had been different, dancing with Patrick Grady, and she'd felt that he found it different dancing with her, although he'd never said so. At night she'd dreamed of him and in the daytime too, while she helped her mother in the kitchen or her father with the cows. Week by week she'd returned to the ballroom, delighting in its pink façade and dancing in the arms of Patrick Grady. Often they'd stood together drinking lemonade, not saying anything, not knowing what to say. She knew he loved her, and she believed then that he would lead her one day from the dim, romantic ballroom, from its blueness and its pinkness and its crystal bowl of light and its music. She believed he would lead her into sunshine, to the town and the Church of Our Lady Queen of Heaven, to marriage and smiling faces. But someone else had got Patrick Grady, a girl from the town who'd never danced in the wayside ballroom. She'd scooped up Patrick Grady when he didn't have a chance.

Bridie had wept, hearing that. By night she'd lain in her bed in the farmhouse, quietly crying, the tears rolling into her hair and making the pillow damp. When she woke in the early morning the thought was still naggingly with her and it remained with her by day, replacing her daytime dreams of happiness. Someone told her later on that he'd crossed to Britain, to Wolverhampton, with the girl he'd married, and she imagined him there, in a place she wasn't able properly to visualize, labouring in a factory, his children being born and acquiring the accent of the area. The Ballroom of Romance wasn't the same without him, and when no one else stood out for her particularly over the years and when no one offered her marriage, she found herself wondering about Dano Ryan. If you couldn't have love, the next best thing was surely a decent man.

Bowser Egan hardly fell into that category, nor did Tim Daly. And it was plain to everyone that Cat Bolger and Madge Dowding were wasting their time over the man with the long arms. Madge Dowding was already a figure of fun in the ballroom, the way she ran after the bachelors; Cat Bolger would end up the same if she wasn't careful. One way or another it wasn't difficult to be a figure of fun in the ballroom, and you didn't have to be as old as Madge Dowding: a girl who'd just left the Presentation Nuns had once asked Eyes Horgan what he had in his trouser pocket and he told her it was a penknife. She'd repeated this afterwards in the cloakroom, how she'd requested Eyes Horgan not to dance so close to her because his penknife was sticking into her. 'Jeez, aren't you the right baby!' Patty Byrne had shouted delightedly; everyone had laughed, knowing that Eyes Horgan only came to the ballroom for stuff like that. He was no use to any girl.

'Two lemonades, Mrs Dwyer,' Bowser Egan said, 'and two packets of Kerry Creams. Is Kerry Creams all right, Bridie?'

She nodded, smiling. Kerry Creams would be fine, she said.

'Well, Bridie, isn't that the great outfit you have!' Mrs Dwyer remarked. 'Doesn't the red suit her, Bowser?'

By the swing-doors stood Mr Dwyer, smoking a cigarette that he held cupped in his left hand. His small eyes noted all developments. He had been aware of Madge Dowding's anxiety when Eyes Horgan had inserted two fingers into the back opening of her dress. He had looked away, not caring for the incident, but had it developed further he would have spoken to Eyes Horgan, as he had on other occasions. Some of the younger lads didn't know any better and would dance very close to their partners, who generally were too embarrassed to do anything about it, being young themselves. But that, in Mr Dwyer's opinion, was a different kettle of fish altogether because they were decent young lads who'd in no time at all be doing a steady line with a girl and would end up as he had himself with Mrs Dwyer, in the same house with her, sleeping in a bed with her, firmly married. It was the middle-aged bachelors who required the watching: they came down from the hills like mountain goats, released from their mammies and from the smell of animals and soil. Mr Dwyer continued to watch Eyes Horgan, wondering how drunk he was.

Dano Ryan's song came to an end, Mr Swanton laid down his clarinet, Mr Maloney rose from the piano. Dano Ryan wiped sweat from his face and the three men slowly moved towards Mrs Dwyer's trestle table.

'Jeez, you have powerful legs,' Eyes Horgan whispered to Madge Dowding, but Madge Dowding's attention was on the man with the long arms, who had left Cat Bolger's side and was proceeding in the direction of the men's lavatory. He never took refreshments. She moved, herself, towards the men's lavatory, to take up a position outside it, but Eyes Horgan followed her. 'Would you take a lemonade, Madge?' he asked. He had a small bottle of whiskey on him: if they went into a corner they could add a drop of it to the lemonade. She didn't drink spirits, she reminded him, and he went away.

'Excuse me a minute,' Bowser Egan said, putting down his bottle of lemonade. He crossed the floor to the lavatory. He too, Bridie knew, would have a small bottle of whiskey on him. She watched while Dano Ryan, listening to a story Mr Maloney was telling, paused in the centre of the ballroom, his head bent to hear what was being said. He was a big man, heavily made, with black hair that was slightly touched with grey, and big hands. He laughed when Mr Maloney came to the end of his story and then bent his head again, in order to listen to a story told by Mr Swanton.

'Are you on your own, Bridie?' Cat Bolger asked, and Bridie said she was waiting for Bowser Egan. 'I think I'll have a lemonade,' Cat Bolger said.

Younger boys and girls stood with their arms still around one another, queuing up for refreshments. Boys who hadn't danced at all, being nervous because they didn't know any steps, stood in groups, smoking and making jokes. Girls who hadn't been danced with yet talked to one another, their eyes wandering. Some of them sucked at straws in lemonade bottles.

Bridie, still watching Dano Ryan, imagined him wearing the glasses he'd referred to, sitting in the farmhouse kitchen, reading one of her father's Wild West novels. She imagined the three of them eating a meal she'd prepared, fried eggs and rashers and fried potato-cakes, and tea and bread and butter and jam, brown bread and soda and shop bread. She imagined Dano Ryan leaving the kitchen in the morning to go out to the fields in order to weed the mangolds, and her father hobbling off behind him, and the two men working together. She saw hay being cut, Dano Ryan with the scythe that she'd learned to use herself, her father using a rake as best he could. She saw herself, because of the extra help, being able to attend to things in the farmhouse, things she'd never had time for because of the cows and the hens and the fields. There were bedroom curtains that needed repairing where the net had ripped, and wallpaper that had become loose and needed to be stuck up with flour paste. The scullery required whitewashing.

The night he'd blown up the tyre of her bicycle she'd thought he was going to kiss her. He'd crouched on the ground in the darkness with his ear to the tyre, listening for escaping air. When he could hear none he'd straightened up and said he thought she'd be all right on the bicycle. His face had been quite close to hers and she'd smiled at him. At that moment, unfortunately, Mr Maloney had blown an impatient blast on the horn of his motor-car.

Often she'd been kissed by Bowser Egan, on the nights when he insisted on riding part of the way home with her. They had to dismount in order to push their bicycles up a hill and the first time he'd accompanied her he'd contrived to fall against her, steadying himself by putting a hand on her shoulder. The next thing she was aware of was the moist quality of his lips and the sound of his bicycle as it clattered noisily on the road. He'd suggested then, regaining his breath, that they should go into a field.

That was nine years ago. In the intervening passage of time she'd been kissed as well, in similar circumstances, by Eyes Horgan and Tim Daly. She'd gone into fields with them and permitted them to put their arms about her while heavily they breathed. At one time or another she had imagined marriage with one or other of them, seeing them in the farmhouse with her father, even though the fantasies were unlikely.

Bridie stood with Cat Bolger, knowing that it would be some time before Bowser Egan came out of the lavatory. Mr Maloney, Mr Swanton and Dano Ryan approached, Mr Maloney insisting that he would fetch three bottles of lemonade from the trestle table.

'You sang the last one beautifully,' Bridie said to Dano Ryan. 'Isn't it a beautiful song?'

Mr Swanton said it was the finest song ever written, and Cat Bolger said she preferred 'Danny Boy', which in her opinion was the finest song ever written.

'Take a suck of that,' said Mr Maloney, handing Dano Ryan and Mr Swanton bottles of lemonade. 'How's Bridie tonight? Is your father well, Bridie?'

Her father was all right, she said.

'I hear they're starting a cement factory,' said Mr Maloney. 'Did anyone hear talk of that? They're after striking some commodity in the earth that makes good cement. Ten feet down, over at Kilmalough.'

'It'll bring employment,' said Mr Swanton. 'It's employment that's necessary in this area.'

'Canon O'Connell was on about it,' Mr Maloney said. 'There's Yankee money involved.'

'Will the Yanks come over?' inquired Cat Bolger. 'Will they run it themselves, Mr Maloney?'

Mr Maloney, intent on his lemonade, didn't hear the questions and Cat Bolger didn't repeat them.

'There's stuff called Optrex,' Bridie said quietly to Dano Ryan, 'that my father took the time he had a cold in his eyes. Maybe Optrex would settle the watering, Dano.'

'Ah sure, it doesn't worry me that much – '

'It's terrible, anything wrong with the eyes. You wouldn't want to take a chance. You'd get Optrex in a chemist, Dano, and a little bowl with it so that you can bathe the eyes.'

Her father's eyes had become red-rimmed and unsightly to look at. She'd gone into Riordan's Medical Hall in the town and had explained what the trouble was, and Mr Riordan had recommended Optrex. She told this to Dano Ryan, adding that her father had had no trouble with his eyes since. Dano Ryan nodded.

'Did you hear that, Mrs Dwyer?' Mr Maloney called out. 'A cement factory for Kilmalough.'

Mrs Dwyer wagged her head, placing empty bottles in a crate. She'd heard references to the cement factory, she said: it was the best news for a long time.

'Kilmalough won't know itself,' her husband commented, joining her in her task with the empty lemonade bottles.

''Twill bring prosperity certainly,' said Mr Swanton. 'I was saying just there, Justin, that employment's what's necessary.'

'Sure, won't the Yanks –' began Cat Bolger, but Mr Maloney interrupted her.

'The Yanks'll be in at the top, Cat, or maybe not here at all – maybe only inserting money into it. It'll be local labour entirely.'

'You'll not marry a Yank, Cat,' said Mr Swanton, loudly laughing. 'You can't catch those fellows.'

'Haven't you plenty of homemade bachelors?' suggested Mr Maloney. He laughed also, throwing away the straw he was sucking through and tipping the bottle into his mouth. Cat Bolger told him to get on with himself. She moved towards the men's lavatory and took up a position outside it, not speaking to Madge Dowding, who was still standing there.

'Keep a watch on Eyes Horgan,' Mrs Dwyer warned her husband, which was advice she gave him at this time every Saturday night, knowing that Eyes Horgan was drinking in the lavatory. When he was drunk Eyes Horgan was the most difficult of the bachelors.

'I have a drop of it left, Dano,' Bridie said quietly. 'I could bring it over on Saturday. The eye stuff.'

'Ah, don't worry yourself, Bridie – '

'No trouble at all. Honestly now – '

'Mrs Griffin has me fixed up for a test with Dr Cready. The old eyes are no worry, only when

I'm reading the paper or at the pictures. Mrs Griffin says I'm only straining them due to lack of glasses.'

He looked away while he said that, and she knew at once that Mrs Griffin was arranging to marry him. She felt it instinctively: Mrs Griffin was going to marry him because she was afraid that if he moved away from her cottage, to get married to someone else, she'd find it hard to replace him with another lodger who'd be good to her affected son. He'd become a father to Mrs Griffin's affected son, to whom already he was kind. It was a natural outcome, for Mrs Grifin had all the chances, seeing him every night and morning and not having to make do with weekly encounters in a ballroom.

She thought of Patrick Grady, seeing in her mind his pale, thin face. She might be the mother of four of his children now, or seven or eight maybe. She might be living in Wolverhampton, going out to the pictures in the evenings, instead of looking after a one-legged man. If the weight of circumstances hadn't intervened she wouldn't be standing in a wayside ballroom, mourning the marriage of a road-mender she didn't love. For a moment she thought she might cry, standing there thinking of Patrick Grady in Wolverhampton. In her life, on the farm and in the house, there was no place for tears. Tears were a luxury, like flowers would be in the fields where the mangolds grew, or fresh whitewash in the scullery. It wouldn't have been fair ever to have wept in the kitchen while her father sat listening to *Spot the Talent*: her father had more right to weep, having lost a leg. He suffered in a greater way, yet he remained kind and concerned for her.

In the Ballroom of Romance she felt behind her eyes the tears that it would have been improper to release in the presence of her father. She wanted to let them go, to feel them streaming on her cheeks, to receive the sympathy of Dano Ryan and of everyone else. She wanted them all to listen to her while she told them about Patrick Grady who was now in Wolverhampton and about the death of her mother and her own life since. She wanted Dano Ryan to put his arm around her so that she could lean her head against it. She wanted him to look at her in his decent way and to stroke with his road-mender's fingers the backs of her hands. She might wake in a bed with him and imagine for a moment that he was Patrick Grady. She might bathe his eyes and pretend.

'Back to business,' said Mr Maloney, leading his band across the floor to their instruments.

'Tell your father I was asking for him,' Dano Ryan said. She smiled and she promised, as though nothing had happened, that she would tell her father that.

She danced with Tim Daly and then again with the youth who'd said he intended to emigrate. She saw Madge Dowding moving swiftly towards the man with the long arms as he came out of the lavatory, moving faster than Cat Bolger. Eyes Horgan approached Cat Bolger. Dancing with her, he spoke earnestly, attempting to persuade her to permit him to ride part of the way home with her. He was unaware of the jealousy that was coming from her as she watched Madge Dowding holding close to her the man with the long arms while they performed a quickstep. Cat Bolger was in her thirties also.

'Get away out of that,' said Bowser Egan, cutting in on the youth who was dancing with Bridie. 'Go home to your mammy, boy.' He took her into his arms, saying again that she was looking great tonight. 'Did you hear about the cement factory?' he said. 'Isn't it great for Kilmalough?'

She agreed. She said what Mr Swanton and Mr Maloney had said: that the cement factory would bring employment to the neighbourhood.

'Will I ride home with you a bit, Bridie?' Bowser Egan suggested, and she pretended not to hear him. 'Aren't you my girl, Bridie, and always have been?' he said, a statement that made no sense at all.

His voice went on whispering at her, saying he would marry her tomorrow only his mother wouldn't permit another woman in the house. She knew what it was like herself, he reminded her, having a parent to look after: you couldn't leave them to rot, you had to honour your father and your mother.

She danced to 'The Bells Are Ringing', moving her legs in time with Bowser Egan's while over his shoulder she watched Dano Ryan softly striking one of his smaller drums. Mrs Griffin had got him even though she was nearly fifty, with no looks at all, a lumpish woman with lumpish legs and arms. Mrs Griffin had got him just as the girl had got Patrick Grady.

The music ceased, Bowser Egan held her hard against him, trying to touch her face with his. Around them, people whistled and clapped: the evening had come to an end. She walked away from Bowser Egan, knowing that not ever again would she dance in the Ballroom of Romance. She'd been a figure of fun, trying to promote a relationship with a middle-aged County Council labourer, as ridiculous as Madge Dowding dancing on beyond her time.

'I'm waiting outside for you, Cat,' Eyes Horgan called out, lighting a cigarette as he made for the swing-doors.

Already the man with the long arms – made long, so they said, from carrying rocks off his land – had left the ballroom. Others were moving briskly. Mr Dwyer was tidying the chairs.

In the cloakroom the girls put on their coats and said they'd see one another at Mass the next day. Madge Dowding hurried. 'Are you OK, Bridie?' Patty Byrne asked and Bridie said she was. She smiled at little Patty Byrne, wondering if a day would come for the younger girl also, if one day she'd decide that she was a figure of fun in a wayside ballroom.

'Good-night so,' Bridie said, leaving the cloak-room, and the girls who were still chatting there wished her good-night. Outside the cloakroom she paused for a moment. Mr Dwyer was still tidying the chairs, picking up empty lemonade bottles from the floor, setting the chairs in a neat row. His wife was sweeping the floor. 'Good-night, Bridie,' Mr Dwyer said. 'Good-night, Bridie,' his wife said.

Extra lights had been switched on so that the Dwyers could see what they were doing. In the glare the blue walls of the ballroom seemed tatty, marked with hair-oil where men had leaned against them, inscribed with names and initials and hearts

with arrows through them. The crystal bowl gave
out a light that was ineffective in the glare; the bowl
was broken here and there, which wasn't noticeable
when the other lights weren't on.

'Good-night so,' Bridie said to the Dwyers. She
passed through the swing-doors and descended the
three concrete steps on the gravel expanse in front of
the ballroom. People were gathered on the gravel,
talking in groups, standing with their bicycles. She
saw Madge Dowding going off with Tim Daly. A
youth rode away with a girl on the crossbar of his
bicycle. The engines of motor-cars started.

'Good-night, Bridie,' Dano Ryan said.

'Good-night, Dano,' she said.

She walked across the gravel towards her bicycle,
hearing Mr Maloney, somewhere behind her, repeating that no matter how you looked at it the
cement factory would be a great thing for Kilmalough. She heard the bang of a car door and knew it
was Mr Swanton banging the door of Mr Maloney's
car because he always gave it the same loud bang.
Two other doors banged as she reached her bicycle
and then the engine started up and the headlights
went on. She touched the two tyres of the bicycle to
make certain she hadn't a puncture. The wheels of
Mr Maloney's car traversed the gravel and were silent
when they reached the road.

'Good-night, Bridie,' someone called, and she
replied, pushing her bicycle towards the road.

'Will I ride a little way with you?' Bowser Egan
asked.

They rode together and when they arrived at the
hill for which it was necessary to dismount she

looked back and saw in the distance the four coloured bulbs that decorated the façade of the Ballroom of Romance. As she watched, the lights went out, and she imagined Mr Dwyer pulling the metal grid across the front of his property and locking the two padlocks that secured it. His wife would be waiting with the evening's takings, sitting in the front of their car.

'D'you know what it is, Bridie,' said Bowser Egan, 'you were never looking better than tonight.' He took from a pocket of his suit the small bottle of whiskey he had. He uncorked it and drank some and then handed it to her. She took it and drank. 'Sure, why wouldn't you?' he said, surprised to see her drinking because she never had in his company before. It was an unpleasant taste, she considered, a taste she'd experienced only twice before, when she'd taken whiskey as a remedy for toothache. 'What harm would it do you?' Bowser Egan said as she raised the bottle again to her lips. He reached out a hand for it, though, suddenly concerned lest she should consume a greater share than he wished her to.

She watched him drinking more expertly than she had. He would always be drinking, she thought. He'd be lazy and useless, sitting in the kitchen with the *Irish Press*. He'd waste money buying a second-hand motor-car in order to drive into the town to go to the public houses on fair-days.

'She's shook these days,' he said, referring to his mother. 'She'll hardly last two years, I'm thinking.' He threw the empty whiskey bottle into the ditch and lit a cigarette. They pushed their bicycles. He said:

'When she goes, Bridie, I'll sell the bloody place up. I'll sell the pigs and the whole damn one and twopence worth.' He paused in order to raise the cigarette to his lips. He drew in smoke and exhaled it. 'With the cash that I'll get I could improve some place else, Bridie.'

They reached a gate on the left-hand side of the road and automatically they pushed their bicycles towards it and leaned them against it. He climbed over the gate into the field and she climbed after him. 'Will we sit down here, Bridie?' he said, offering the suggestion as one that had just occurred to him, as though they'd entered the field for some other purpose.

'We could improve a place like your own one,' he said, putting his right arm around her shoulders. 'Have you a kiss in you, Bridie?' He kissed her, exerting pressure with his teeth. When his mother died he would sell his farm and spend the money in the town. After that he would think of getting married because he'd have nowhere to go, because he'd want a fire to sit at and a woman to cook food for him. He kissed her again, his lips hot, the sweat on his cheeks sticking to her. 'God, you're great at kissing,' he said.

She rose, saying it was time to go, and they climbed over the gate again. 'There's nothing like a Saturday,' he said. 'Good-night to you so, Bridie.'

He mounted his bicycle and rode down the hill, and she pushed hers to the top and then mounted it also. She rode through the night as on Saturday nights for years she had ridden and never would ride again because she'd reached a certain age. She would wait now and in time Bowser Egan would seek her out because his mother would have died. Her father would probably have died also by then. She would marry Bowser Egan because it would be lonesome being by herself in the farmhouse.

The Grass Widows

The headmaster of a great English public school visited every summer a village in County Galway for the sake of the fishing in a number of nearby rivers. For more than forty years this stern, successful man had brought his wife to the Slieve Gashal Hotel, a place, so he said, he had come to love. A smiling man called Mr Doyle had been for all the headmaster's experience of the hotel its obliging proprietor: Mr Doyle had related stories to the headmaster late at night in the hotel bar, after the headmaster's wife had retired to bed; they had discussed together the fruitfulness of the local rivers, although in truth Mr Doyle had never held a rod in his life. 'You feel another person,' the headmaster had told generations of his pupils, 'among blue mountains, in the quiet little hotel.' On walks through the school grounds with a senior boy on either side of him he had spoken of the soft peace of the riverside and of the unrivalled glory of being alone with one's mind. He talked to his boys of Mr Doyle and his unassuming ways, and of the little village that was a one-horse place and none the worse for that, and of the good plain food that came from the Slieve Gashal's kitchen.

To Jackson Major the headmaster enthused during all the year that Jackson Major was head

boy of the famous school, and Jackson Major did
not ever forget the paradise that then had formed in
his mind. 'I know a place,' he said to his fiancée
long after he had left the school, 'that's perfect for
our honeymoon.' He told her about the heathery
hills that the headmaster had recalled for him, and
the lakes and rivers and the one-horse little village
in which, near a bridge, stood the ivy-covered bulk
of the Slieve Gashal Hotel. 'Lovely, darling,'
murmured the bride-to-be of Jackson Major, thinking at the time of a clock in the shape of a human
hand that someone had given them and which
would naturally have to be changed for something
else. She'd been hoping that he would suggest
Majorca for their honeymoon, but if he wished to
go to this other place she didn't intend to make a
fuss. 'Idyllic for a honeymoon,' the headmaster had
once remarked to Jackson Major, and Jackson
Major had not forgotten. *Steady but unimaginative*
were words that had been written of him on a
school report.

The headmaster, a square, bald man with a head
that might have been carved from oak, a man who
wore rimless spectacles and whose name was Angusthorpe, discovered when he arrived at the Slieve
Gashal Hotel in the summer of 1968 that in the
intervening year a tragedy had occurred. It had
become the custom of Mr Angusthorpe to book
his fortnight's holiday by saying simply to Mr Doyle:
'Till next year then,' an anticipation that Mr Doyle
would translate into commercial terms, reserving the
same room for the headmaster and his wife in twelve
months' time. No letters changed hands during the

year, no confirmation of the booking was ever
necessary: Mr Angusthorpe and his wife arrived
each summer after the trials of the school term,
knowing that their room would be waiting for
them, with sweet-peas in a vase in the window,
and Mr Doyle full of welcome in the hall. 'He died
in Woolworth's in Galway,' said Mr Doyle's son in
the summer of 1968. 'He was buying a shirt at the
time.'

Afterwards, Mr Angusthorpe said to his wife that
when Mr Doyle's son spoke those words he knew
that nothing was ever going to be the same again.
Mr Doyle's son, known locally as Scut Doyle, went
on speaking while the headmaster and his small
wife, grey-haired, and bespectacled also, stood in
the hall. He told them that he had inherited the
Slieve Gashal and that for all his adult life he had
been employed in the accounts department of a
paper-mill in Dublin. 'I thought at first I'd sell the
place up,' he informed the Angusthorpes, 'and then
I thought maybe I'd attempt to make a go of it.
"Will we have a shot at it?" I said to the wife, and
God bless her, she said why wouldn't I?' While he
spoke, the subject of his last remarks appeared
behind him in the hall, a woman whose appearance did not at all impress Mr Angusthorpe. She
was pale-faced and fat and, so Mr Angusthorpe
afterwards suggested to his wife, sullen. She stood
silently by her husband, whose appearance did not
impress Mr Angusthorpe either, since the new
proprietor of the Slieve Gashal, a man with shaking hands and a cocky grin, did not appear to have
shaved himself that day. 'One or other of them, if

not both,' said Mr Angusthorpe afterwards, 'smelt of drink.'

The Angusthorpes were led to their room by a girl whose age Mr Angusthorpe estimated to be thirteen. 'What's become of Joseph?' he asked her as they mounted the stairs, referring to an old porter who had always in the past been spick-and-span in a uniform, but the child seemed not to understand the question, for she offered it no reply. In the room there were no sweet-peas, and although they had entered by a door that was familiar to them, the room itself was greatly altered: it was, to begin with, only half the size it had been before. 'Great heavens!' exclaimed Mr Angusthorpe, striking a wall with his fist and finding it to be a partition. 'He had the carpenters in,' the child said.

Mr Angusthorpe, in a natural fury, descended the stairs and shouted in the hall. 'Mr Doyle!' he called out in his peremptory headmaster's voice. 'Mr Doyle! Mr Doyle!'

Doyle emerged from the back regions of the hotel, with a cigarette in his mouth. There were feathers on his clothes, and he held in his right hand a half-plucked chicken. In explanation he said that he had been giving his wife a hand. She was not herself, he confided to Mr Angusthorpe, on account of it being her bad time of the month.

'Our room,' protested Mr Angusthorpe. 'We can't possibly sleep in a tiny space like that. You've cut the room in half, Mr Doyle.'

Doyle nodded. All the bedrooms in the hotel, he told Mr Angusthorpe, had been divided, since they were uneconomical otherwise. He had spent four

hundred and ten pounds having new doorways made
and putting on new wallpaper. He began to go into
the details of this expense, plucking feathers from the
chicken as he stood there. Mr Angusthorpe coldly
remarked that he had not booked a room in which
you couldn't swing a cat.

'Excuse me, sir,' interrupted Doyle. 'You booked
a room a year ago: you did not reserve a specific
room. D'you know what I mean, Mr Angusthorpe? I
have no note that you specified with my father to
have the exact room again.'

'It was an understood thing between us – '

'My father unfortunately died.'

Mr Angusthorpe regarded the man, disliking him
intensely. It occurred to him that he had never in
his life carried on a conversation with a hotel
proprietor who held in his right hand a half-
plucked chicken and whose clothes had feathers
on them. His inclination was to turn on his heel
and march with his wife from the unsatisfactory
hotel, telling, if need be, this unprepossessing
individual to go to hell. Mr Angusthorpe thought
of doing that, but then he wondered where he and
his wife could go. Hotels in the area were notor-
iously full at this time of year, in the middle of the
fishing season.

'I must get on with this for the dinner,' said Doyle,
'or the wife will be having me guts for garters.' He
winked at Mr Angusthorpe, flicking a quantity of
cigarette ash from the pale flesh of the chicken. He
left Mr Angusthorpe standing there.

The child had remained with Mrs Angusthorpe
while the headmaster had sought an explanation

downstairs. She had stood silently by the door until
Mrs Angusthorpe, fearing a violent reaction on the
part of her husband if he discovered the child present
when he returned, suggested that she should go
away. But the child had taken no notice of that
and Mrs Angusthorpe, being unable to think of
anything else to say, had asked her at what time of
year old Mr Doyle had died. 'The funeral was ten
miles long, missus,' replied the child. 'Me father
wasn't sober till the Monday.' Mr Angusthorpe,
returning, asked the child sharply why she was
lingering and the child explained that she was waiting to be tipped. Mr Angusthorpe gave her a
threepenny-piece.

In the partitioned room, which now had a pink
wallpaper on the walls and an elaborate frieze from
which flowers of different colours cascaded down
the four corners, the Angusthorpes surveyed their
predicament. Mr Angusthorpe told his wife the
details of his interview with Doyle, and when he
had talked for twenty minutes he came more
definitely to the conclusion that the best thing
they could do would be to remain for the
moment. The rivers could hardly have altered,
he was thinking, and that the hotel was now
more than inadequate was a consequence that
would affect his wife more than it would affect
him. In the past she had been wont to spend her
days going for a brief walk in the morning and
returning to the pleasant little dining-room for a
solitary lunch, and then sleeping or reading until it
was time for a cup of tea, after which she would
again take a brief walk. She was usually sitting by

the fire in the lounge when he returned from his
day's excursion. Perhaps all that would be less
attractive now, Mr Angusthorpe thought, but
there was little he could do about it and it was
naturally only fair that they should at least remain
for a day or two.

That night the dinner was well below the standard
of the dinners they had in the past enjoyed in the
Slieve Gashal. Mrs Angusthorpe was unable to
consume her soup because there were quite large
pieces of bone and gristle in it. The headmaster
laughed over his prawn cocktail because, he said, it
tasted of absolutely nothing at all. He had recovered
from his initial shock and was now determined that
the hotel must be regarded as a joke. He eyed his
wife's plate of untouched soup, saying it was better to
make the best of things. Chicken and potatoes and
mashed turnip were placed before them by a nervous
woman in the uniform of a waitress. Turnip made
Mrs Angusthorpe sick in the stomach, even the sight
of it: at another time in their life her husband might
have remembered and ordered the vegetable from
the table, but what he was more intent upon now
was discovering if the Slieve Gashal still possessed a
passable hock, which surprisingly it did. After a few
glasses, he said:

'We'll not come next year, of course. While I'm
out with the rod, my dear, you might scout around
for another hotel.'

They never brought their car with them, the
headmaster's theory being that the car was something they wished to escape from. Often she had
thought it might be nice to have a car at the Slieve

Gashal so that she could drive around the country-
side during the day, but she saw his argument and
had never pressed her view. Now, it seemed, he
was suggesting that she should scout about for
another hotel on foot.

'No, no,' he said. 'There is an excellent bus
service in Ireland.' He spoke with a trace of
sarcasm, as though she should have known that
no matter what else he expected of her, he did not
expect her to tramp about the roads looking for
another hotel. He gave a little laugh, leaving the
matter vaguely with her, his eyes like the eyes of a
fish behind his rimless spectacles. Boys had feared
him and disliked him too, some even had hated
him; yet others had been full of a respect that
seemed at times like adoration. As she struggled
with her watery turnips she could sense that his
mind was quite made up: he intended to remain
for the full fortnight in the changed hotel because
the lure of the riverside possessed him too strongly
to consider an alternative.

'I might find a place we could move to,' she said.
'I mean, in a day or so.'

'They'll all be full, my dear.' He laughed without
humour in his laugh, not amused by anything. 'We
must simply grin and bear it. The chicken,' he added,
'might well have been worse.'

'Excuse me,' Mrs Angusthorpe said, and quickly
rose from the table and left the dining-room. From a
tape-recorder somewhere dance music began to play.

'Is the wife all right?' Doyle asked Mr Angusthorpe,
coming up and sitting down in the chair she had
vacated. He had read in a hotelier's journal that tourists

enjoyed a friendly atmosphere and the personal attention of the proprietor.

'We've had a long day,' responded the headmaster
genially enough.

'Ah well, of course you have.'

The dining-room was full, indicating that business
was still brisk in the hotel. Mr Angusthorpe had
noted a familiar face or two and had made dignified
salutations. These people would surely have walked
out if the hotel was impossible in all respects.

'At her time of the month,' Doyle was saying, 'the
wife gets as fatigued as an old horse. Like your own
one, she's gone up to her bed already.'

'My wife – '

'Ah, I wasn't suggesting Mrs Angusthorpe, was
that way at all. They have fatigue in common
tonight, sir, that's all I meant.'

Doyle appeared to be drunk. There was a bleari-
ness about his eyes that suggested inebriation to
Mr Angusthorpe, and his shaking hands might well
be taken as a sign of repeated over-indulgence.

'She wakes up at two a.m. as lively as a bird,' said
Doyle. 'She's keen for a hug and a pat – '

'Quite so,' interrupted Mr Angusthorpe quickly.
He looked unpleasantly at his unwelcome companion. He allowed his full opinion of the man to
pervade his glance.

'Well, I'll be seeing you,' said Doyle, rising and
seeming to be undismayed. 'I'll tell the wife you were
asking for her,' he added with a billowing laugh,
before moving on to another table.

Shortly after that, Mr Angusthorpe left the
dining-room, having resolved that he would not

relate this conversation to his wife. He would avoid Doyle in the future, he promised himself, and when by chance they did meet he would make it clear that he did not care to hear his comments on any subject. It was a pity that the old man had died and that all this nastiness had grown up in his place, but there was nothing whatsoever that might be done about it and at least the weather looked good. He entered the bar and dropped into conversation with a man he had met several times before, a solicitor from Dublin, a bachelor called Gorman.

'I was caught the same way,' Mr Gorman said, 'only everywhere else is full. It's the end of the Slieve Gashal, you know: the food's inedible.'

He went on to relate a series of dishes that had already been served during his stay, the most memorable of which appeared to be a rabbit stew that had had a smell of ammonia. 'There's margarine every time instead of butter, and some queer type of marmalade in the morning: it has a taste of tin to it. The same mashed turnip,' said Gorman, 'is the only vegetable he offers.'

The headmaster changed the subject, asking how the rivers were. The fishing was better than ever he'd known it, Mr Gorman reported, and he retailed experiences to prove the claim. 'Isn't it all that matters in the long run?' suggested Mr Gorman, and Mr Angusthorpe readily agreed that it was. He would refrain from repeating to his wife the information about the marmalade that tasted of tin, or the absence of variation where vegetables were concerned. He left the bar at nine o'clock, determined to slip quietly into bed without disturbing her.

In the middle of that night, at midnight precisely, the Angusthorpes were awakened simultaneously by a noise from the room beyond the new partition.

'Put a pillow down, darling,' a male voice was saying as clearly as if its possessor stood in the room beside the Angusthorpes' bed.

'Couldn't we wait until another time?' a woman pleaded in reply. 'I don't see what good a pillow will do.'

'It'll lift you up a bit,' the man explained. 'It said in the book to put a pillow down if there was difficulty.'

'I don't see – '

'It'll make entry easier,' said the man. 'It's a well-known thing.'

Mrs Angusthorpe switched on her bedside light and saw that her husband was pretending to be asleep. 'I'm going to rap on the wall,' she whispered. 'It's disgusting, listening to this.'

'I think I'm going down,' said the man.

'My God,' whispered Mr Angusthorpe, opening his eyes. 'It's Jackson Major.'

At breakfast, Mrs Angusthorpe ate margarine on her toast and the marmalade that had a taste of tin. She did not say anything. She watched her husband cutting into a fried egg on a plate that bore the marks of the waitress's two thumbs. Eventually he placed his knife and fork together on the plate and left them there.

For hours they had lain awake, listening to the conversation beyond the inadequate partition. The newly wed wife of Jackson Major had wept and said that Jackson had better divorce her at once. She had designated the hotel they were in as a frightful place, fit only for Irish tinkers. 'That filthy meal!' the wife of Jackson Major had cried emotionally. 'That awful drunk man!' And Jackson Major had apologized and had mentioned Mr Angusthorpe by name, wondering what on earth his old headmaster could ever have seen in such an establishment. 'Let's try again,' he had suggested, and the Angusthorpes had listened to a repetition of Mrs Jackson's unhappy tears. 'How can you rap on the wall?' Mr Angusthorpe had angrily whispered. 'How can we even admit that conversation can be heard? Jackson was head boy.'

'In the circumstances,' said Mrs Angusthorpe at breakfast, breaking the long silence, 'it would be better to leave.'

He knew it would be. He knew that on top of everything else the unfortunate fact that Jackson Major was in the room beyond the partition and would sooner or later discover that the partition was far from sound-proof could be exceedingly embarrassing in view of what had taken place during the night. There was, as well, the fact that he had enthused so eloquently to Jackson Major about the hotel that Jackson Major had clearly, on his word alone, brought his bride there. He had even said, he recalled, that the Slieve Gashal would be ideal for a honeymoon. Mr Angusthorpe considered all that, yet could not forget his forty years' experience of

the surrounding rivers, or the information of
Mr Gorman that the rivers this year were better
than ever.

'We could whisper,' he suggested in what was
itself a whisper. 'We could whisper in our room so
that they wouldn't know you can hear.'

'Whisper?' she said. She shook her head.

She remembered days in the rain, walking about
the one-horse village with nothing whatsoever to do
except to walk about, or lie on her bed reading
detective stories. She remembered listening to his
reports of his day and feeling sleepy listening to them.
She remembered thinking, once or twice, that it had
never occurred to him that what was just a change
and a rest for her could not at all be compared to the
excitements he derived from his days on the river-
bank, alone with his mind. He was a great, successful
man, big and square and commanding, with the cold
eyes of the fish he sought in mountain rivers. He had
made a firm impression on generations of boys, and
on parents and governors, and often on a more
general public, yet he had never been able to give
her children. She had needed children because she
was, compared with him, an unimportant kind of
person.

She thought of him in Chapel, gesturing at six
hundred boys from the pulpit, in his surplice and
red academic hood, releasing words from his throat
that were as cold as ice and cleverly made sense.
She thought of a time he had expelled two boys,
when he had sat with her in their drawing-room
waiting for a bell to ring. When the chiming had
ceased he had risen and gone without a word from

the room, his oaken face pale with suppressed
emotion. She knew he saw in the crime of the
two boys a failure on his part, yet he never
mentioned it to her. He had expelled the boys in
public, castigating them with bitterness in his tone,
hating them and hating himself, yet rising above his
shame at having failed with them: dignity was his
greatest ally.

She sat with him once a week at the high table in
the dining-hall surrounded by his prefects, who
politely chatted to her. She remembered Jackson
Major, a tall boy with short black hair who would
endlessly discuss with her husband a web of school
affairs. 'The best head boy I remember,' her husband's voice said again, coming back to her over a
number of years: 'I made no mistake with Jackson.'
Jackson Major had set a half-mile record that
remained unbroken to this day. There had been a
complaint from some child's mother, she recalled,
who claimed that her son had been, by Jackson
Major, too severely caned. *We must not forget*, her
husband had written to that mother, *that your son
almost caused another boy to lose an eye. It was for that
carelessness that he was punished. He bears no resentment:
boys seldom do.*

Yet now this revered, feared and clever man was
suggesting that they should whisper for a fortnight
in their bedroom, so that the couple next door
might not feel embarrassment, so that he himself
might remain in a particularly uncomfortable hotel
in order to fish. It seemed to Mrs Angusthorpe that
there were limits to the role he had laid down for
her and which for all her married life she had

ungrudgingly accepted. She hadn't minded being bored for this fortnight every year, but now he was asking more than that she could continue to feel bored; he was asking her to endure food that made her sick, and to conduct absurd conversations in their bedroom.

'No,' she said, 'we could not whisper.'

'I meant it only for kindness. Kindness to them, you see – '

'You have compensations here. I have none, you know.'

He looked sharply at her, as at an erring new boy who had not yet learnt the ways of school.

'I think we should leave at once,' she said. 'After breakfast.'

That suggestion, he pointed out to her, was nonsensical. They had booked a room in the hotel: they were obliged to pay for it. He was exhausted, he added, after a particularly trying term.

'It's what I'd like,' she said.

He spread margarine on his toast and added to it some of the marmalade. 'We must not be selfish,' he said, suggesting that both of them were on the point of being selfish and that together they must prevent themselves.

'I'd be happier,' she began, but he swiftly interrupted her, reminding her that his holiday had been spoilt enough already and that he for his part was intent on making the best of things. 'Let's simply enjoy what we can,' he said, 'without making a fuss about it.'

At that moment Jackson Major and his wife, a pretty, pale-haired girl called Daphne, entered the

dining-room. They stood at the door, endeavouring
to catch the eye of a waitress, not sure about where
to sit. Mrs Jackson indicated a table that was occupied
by two men, reminding her husband that they had sat
at it last night for dinner. Jackson Major looked
towards it and looked impatiently away, seeming
annoyed with his wife for bothering to draw his
attention to a table at which they clearly could not
sit. It was then, while still annoyed, that he noticed
the Angusthorpes.

Mrs Angusthorpe saw him murmuring to his
wife. He led the way to their table, and
Mrs Angusthorpe observed that his wife moved
less eagerly than he.

'How marvellous, sir,' Jackson Major said, shaking
his headmaster by the hand. Except for a neat
moustache, he had changed hardly at all,
Mrs Angusthorpe noticed; a little fatter in the face,
perhaps, and the small pimples that had marked his
chin as a schoolboy had now cleared up completely.
He introduced his wife to the headmaster, and then
he turned to Mrs Angusthorpe and asked her how
she was. Forgetfully, he omitted to introduce his wife
to her, but she, in spite of that, smiled and nodded at
his wife.

'I'm afraid it's gone down awfully, Jackson,'
Mr Angusthorpe said. 'The hotel's changed hands,
you know. We weren't aware ourselves.'

'It seems quite comfortable, sir,' Jackson Major
said, sitting down and indicating that his wife should
do the same.

'The food was nice before,' said Mrs Angusthorpe.
'It's really awful now.'

'Oh, I wouldn't say awful, dear,' Mr Angusthorpe corrected her. 'One becomes used to a hotel,' he explained to Jackson Major. 'Any change is rather noticeable.'

'We had a perfectly ghastly dinner,' Daphne Jackson said.

'Still,' said Mr Angusthorpe, as though she had not spoken, 'we'll not return another year. My wife is going to scout around for a better place. You've brought your rod, Jackson?'

'Well, yes, I did. I thought that maybe if Daphne felt tired I might once or twice try out your famous rivers, sir.'

Mr Angusthorpe saw Mrs Jackson glance in surprise at her new husband, and she deduced that Mrs Jackson hadn't been aware that a fishing-rod had comprised part of her husband's luggage.

'Capital,' cried Mr Angusthorpe, while the waitress took the Jacksons' order for breakfast. 'You could scout round together,' he said, addressing the two women at once, 'while I show Jackson what's what.'

'It's most kind of you, sir,' Jackson Major said, 'but I think, you know – '

'Capital,' cried Mr Angusthorpe again, his eyes swivelling from face to face, forbidding defiance. He laughed his humourless laugh and he poured himself more tea. 'I told you, dear,' he said to Mrs Angusthorpe. 'There's always a silver lining.'

In the hall of the Slieve Gashal Doyle took a metal stand from beneath the reception desk and busied himself arranging picture postcards on it. His wife had bought the stand in Galway, getting it at a reduced price because it was broken. He was at the moment offended with his wife because of her attitude when he had entered the hotel kitchen an hour ago with a number of ribs of beef. 'Did you drop that meat?' she had said in a harsh voice, looking up from the table where she was making bread. 'Is that dirt on the suet?' He had replied that he'd been obliged to cross the village street hurriedly, to avoid a man on a bicycle. 'You dropped the meat on the road,' she accused. 'D'you want to poison the bloody lot of them?' Feeling hard done by, he had left the kitchen.

While he continued to work with the postcards, Mr Angusthorpe and Jackson Major passed before him with their fishing-rods. 'We'll be frying to-night,' he observed jollily, wagging his head at their two rods. They did not reply: weren't they the queer-looking eejits, he thought, with their sporty clothes and the two tweed hats covered with artificial flies. 'I'll bring it up, sir,' Jackson Major was saying, 'at the Old Boys' Dinner in the autumn.' It was ridiculous, Doyle reflected, going to that much trouble to catch a few fish when all you had to do was to go out at night and shine a torch into the water. 'Would you be interested in postcards, gentlemen?' he inquired, but so absorbed were Mr Angusthorpe and Jackson Major in their conversation that again neither of them made a reply.

Some time later, Daphne Jackson descended the stairs of the hotel. Doyle watched her, admiring her slender legs and the flowered dress she was wearing.

A light-blue cardigan hung casually from her shoulders, its sleeves not occupied by her arms. Wouldn't it be great, he thought, to be married to a young body like that? He imagined her in a bedroom, taking off her cardigan and then her dress. She stood in her underclothes; swiftly she lifted them from her body.

'Would you be interested in postcards at all?' inquired Doyle. 'I have the local views here.'

Daphne smiled at him. Without much interest, she examined the cards on the stand, and then she moved towards the entrance door.

'There's a lovely dinner we have for you today,' said Doyle. 'Ribs of beef that I'm just after handing over to the wife. As tender as an infant.'

He held the door open for her, talking all the time, since he knew they liked to be talked to. He asked her if she was going for a walk and told her that a walk would give her a healthy appetite. The day would keep good, he promised; he had read it in the paper.

'Thank you,' she said.

She walked through a sunny morning that did little to raise her spirits. Outside the hotel there was a large expanse of green grass, bounded on one side by the short village street. She crossed an area of the grass and then passed the butcher's shop in which earlier Doyle had purchased the ribs of beef. She glanced in and the butcher smiled and waved at her, as though he knew her well. She smiled shyly back. Outside a small public house a man was mending a bicycle, which was upturned on the pavement: a child pushing a pram spoke to the man and he spoke to her. Farther on, past a row of cottages, a woman pumped water into a bucket from a green pump at the road's edge, and beyond it, coming towards her slowly, she recognized the figure of Mrs Angusthorpe.

'So we are grass widows,' said Mrs Angusthorpe when she had arrived at a point at which it was suitable to speak.

'Yes.'

'I'm afraid it's our fault, for being here. My husband's, I mean, and mine.'

'My husband could have declined to go fishing.'

The words were sour. They were sour and icy, Mrs Angusthorpe thought, matching her own mood. On her brief walk she had that morning disliked her husband more than ever she had disliked him before, and there was venom in her now. Once upon a time he might at least have heard her desires with what could even have been taken for understanding. He would not have acted upon her desires, since it was not in his nature to do so, but he would not have been guilty, either, of announcing in so obviously false a way that they should enjoy what they could and not make a fuss. There had been a semblance of chivalry in the attitude from which, at the beginning of their marriage, he had briefly regarded her; but forty-seven years had efficiently disposed of that garnish of politeness. A week or so ago a boy at the school had been casual with her, but the headmaster, hearing her report of the matter, had denied that what she stated could ever have occurred: he had moulded the boy in question, he pointed out, he had taken a special interest in the boy because he recognized in him qualities that were admirable: she was touchy, the headmaster said, increasingly touchy these days. She remembered in the first year of their marriage a way he had of patiently leaning back in his chair, puffing at the pipe he affected in those days and listening to her, seeming actually to weigh her arguments against his own. It was a long time now since he had weighed an argument of hers, or even devoted a moment of passing consideration to it. It was a long time since he could possibly have been concerned as to whether or not she found the food in a hotel unpalatable. She was angry when she thought of it this morning, not because she was unused to these circumstances of her life but because, quite suddenly, she had seen her state of resignation as an insult to the woman she once, too long ago, had been.

'I would really like to talk to you,' Mrs Angusthorpe said, to Daphne Jackson's surprise. 'It might be worth your while to stroll back to that hotel with me.'

On her short, angry walk she had realized, too, that once she had greatly disliked Jackson Major because he reminded her in some ways of her husband. A priggish youth, she had recalled, a tedious bore of a boy who had shown her husband a ridiculous respect while also fearing and resembling him. On her walk she had remembered the day he had broken the half-mile record, standing in the sports field in his running clothes, deprecating his effort because he knew his headmaster would wish him to act like that. What

good was winning a half-mile race if he upset his
wife the first time he found himself in a bedroom
with her?

'I remember your husband as a boy,' said
Mrs Angusthorpe. 'He set an athletic record which
has not yet been broken.'

'Yes, he told me.'

'He had trouble with his chin. Pimples that
wouldn't go away. I see all that's been overcome.'

'Well, yes – '

'And trouble also because he beat a boy too hard.
The mother wrote, enclosing the opinion of a
doctor.'

Daphne frowned. She ceased to walk. She stared at
Mrs Angusthorpe.

'Oh yes,' said Mrs Angusthorpe.

They passed the butcher's shop, from the doorway of which the butcher now addressed them.
The weather was good, the butcher said: it was a
suitable time for a holiday. Mrs Angusthorpe
smiled at him and bowed. Daphne, frowning
still, passed on.

'You're right,' Mrs Angusthorpe said next, 'when
you say that your husband could have declined to go
fishing.'

'I think he felt – '

'Odd, I thought, to have a fishing-rod with him in
the first place. Odd on a honeymoon.'

They entered the hotel. Doyle came forward to
meet them. 'Ah, so you've palled up?' he said. 'Isn't
that grand?'

'We could have sherry,' Mrs Angusthorpe suggested, 'in the bar.'

'Of course you could,' said Doyle. 'Won't your two husbands be pegging away at the old fish for the entire day?'

'They promised to be back for lunch,' Daphne said quickly, her voice seeming to herself to be unduly weak. She cleared her throat and remarked to Doyle that the village was pretty. She didn't really wish to sit in the hotel bar drinking sherry with the wife of her husband's headmaster. It was all ridiculous, she thought, on a honeymoon.

'Go down into the bar,' said Doyle, 'and I'll be down myself in a minute.'

Mrs Angusthorpe seized with the fingers of her left hand the flowered material of Daphne's dress. 'The bar's down here,' she said, leading the way without releasing her hold.

They sat at a table on which there were a number of absorbent mats that advertised brands of beer. Doyle brought them two glasses of sherry, which Mrs Angusthorpe ordered him to put down to her husband's account. 'Shout out when you're in need of a refill,' he invited. 'I'll be up in the hall.'

'The partition between our bedrooms is far from soundproof,' said Mrs Angusthorpe when Doyle had gone. 'We were awakened in the night.'

'Awakened?'

'As if you were in the room beside us, we heard a conversation.'

'My God!'

'Yes.'

Blood rushed to Daphne Jackson's face. She was aware of an unpleasant sensation in her stomach. She turned her head away. Mrs Angusthorpe said:

'People don't speak out. All my married life, for instance, I haven't spoken out. My dear, you're far too good for Jackson Major.'

It seemed to Daphne, who had been Daphne Jackson for less than twenty-four hours, that the wife of her husband's headmaster was insane. She gulped at the glass of sherry before her, unable to prevent herself from vividly recalling the awfulness of the night before in the small bedroom. He had come at her as she was taking off her blouse. His right hand had shot beneath her underclothes, pressing at her and gripping her. All during their inedible dinner he had been urging her to drink whiskey and wine, and drinking quantities of both himself. In bed he had suddenly become calmer, remembering instructions read in a book.

'Pack a suitcase,' said Mrs Angusthorpe, 'and go.'

The words belonged to a nightmare and Daphne was aware of wishing that she were asleep and dreaming. The memory of tension on her wedding-day, and of guests standing around in sunshine in a London garden, and then the flight by plane, were elements that confused her mind as she listened to this small woman. The tension had been with her as she walked towards the altar and had been with her, too, in her parents' garden. Nor had it eased when she escaped with her husband on a Viscount: it might even have increased on the flight and on the train to Galway, and then in the hired car that had carried her to the small village. It had certainly increased while she attempted to eat stringy chicken at a late hour in the dining-room, while her husband smiled at her and talked about

intoxicants. The reason he had talked so much
about whiskey and wine, she now concluded, was
because he'd been aware of the tension that was
coiled within her.

'You have made a mistake,' came the voice of
Mrs Angusthorpe, 'but even now it is not too late to
rectify it. Do not accept it, reject your error,
Mrs Jackson.'

Doyle came into the bar and brought to them,
without their demanding it, more sherry in two new
glasses. Daphne heard him remarking that the brand
of sherry was very popular in these parts. It was
Spanish sherry, he said, since he would stock nothing
else. He talked about Spain and Spaniards, saying that
at the time of the Spanish Armada Spanish sailors had
been wrecked around the nearby coast.

'I love my husband,' Daphne said when Doyle had
gone again.

She had met her husband in the Hurlingham
Club. He had partnered her in tennis and they had
danced together at a charity dance. She'd listened
while he talked one evening, telling her that the
one thing he regretted was that he hadn't played
golf as a child. Golf was a game, he'd said, that
must be started when young if one was ever to
achieve championship distinction. With tennis that
wasn't quite so important, but it was, of course, as
well to start tennis early also. She had thought he
was rather nice. There was something about his
distant manner that attracted her; there was a
touch of arrogance in the way he didn't look at
her when he spoke. She'd make him look at her,
she vowed.

'My dear,' said Mrs Angusthorpe, 'I've seen the seamy side of Jackson Major. The more I think of him the more I can recall. He forced his way up that school, snatching at chances that weren't his to take, putting himself first, like he did in the half-mile race. There was cruelty in Jackson Major's eye, and ruthlessness and dullness. Like my husband, he has no sense of humour.'

'Mrs Angusthorpe, I really can't listen to this. I was married yesterday to a man I'm in love with. It'll be all right – '

'Why will it be all right?'

'Because,' snapped Daphne Jackson with sudden spirit, 'I shall ask my husband as soon as he returns to take me at once from this horrible hotel. My marriage does not concern you, Mrs Angusthorpe.'

'They are talking now on a riverside, whispering maybe so as not to disturb their prey. They are murmuring about the past, of achievements on the sports field and marches undertaken by a cadet force. While you and I are having a different kind of talk.'

'What our husbands are saying to one another, Mrs Angusthorpe, may well make more sense.'

'What they are not saying is that two women in the bar of this hotel are unhappy. They have forgotten about the two women: they are more relaxed and contented than ever they are with us.'

Mrs Angusthorpe, beady-eyed as she spoke, saw the effect of her words reflected in the uneasy face of the woman beside her. She felt herself carried away by this small triumph, she experienced a headiness that was blissful. She saw in her mind another scene, imagining herself, over lunch, telling

her husband about the simple thing that had
happened. She would watch him sitting there in
all his dignity: she would wait until he was about to
pass a forkful of food to his mouth and then she
would say: 'Jackson Major's wife has left him
already.' And she would smile at him.

'You walked across the dining-room at breakfast,'
said Mrs Angusthorpe. 'An instinct warned me then
that you'd made an error.'

'I haven't made an error. I've told you,
Mrs Angusthorpe – '

'Time will erode the polish of politeness. One day
soon you'll see amusement in his eyes when you
offer an opinion.'

'Please stop, Mrs Angusthorpe. I must go away if
you continue like this – '

'"This man's a bore," you'll suddenly say to
yourself, and look at him amazed.'

'Mrs Angusthorpe – '

'Amazed that you could ever have let it happen.'

'Oh God, please stop,' cried Daphne, tears coming
suddenly from her eyes, her hands rushing to her
cheeks.

'Don't be a silly girl,' whispered Mrs Angusthorpe,
grasping the arm of her companion and tightening
her fingers on it until Daphne felt pain. She thought
as she felt it that Mrs Angusthorpe was a poisonous
woman. She struggled to keep back further tears, she
tried to wrench her arm away.

'I'll tell the man Doyle to order you a car,' said
Mrs Angusthorpe. 'It'll take you into Galway. I'll
lend you money, Mrs Jackson. By one o'clock
tonight you could be sitting in your bed at home,

eating from a tray that your mother brought you. A divorce will come through and one day you'll meet a man who'll love you with a tenderness.'

'My husband loves me, Mrs Angusthorpe – '

'Your husband should marry a woman who's keen on horses or golf, a woman who might take a whip to him, being ten years older than himself. My dear, you're like me: you're a delicate person.'

'Please let go my arm. You've no right to talk to me like this – '

'He is my husband's creature, my husband moulded him. The best head boy he'd ever known, he said to me.'

Daphne, calmer now, did not say anything. She felt the pressure on her arm being removed. She stared ahead of her, at a round mat on the table that advertised Celebration Ale. Without wishing to and perhaps, she thought, because she was so upset, she saw herself suddenly as Mrs Angusthorpe had suggested, sitting up in her own bedroom with a tray of food on her knees and her mother standing beside her, saying it was all right. 'I suddenly realized,' she heard herself saying. 'He took me to this awful hotel, where his old headmaster was. He gave me wine and whiskey, and then in bed I thought I might be sick.' Her mother replied to her, telling her that it wasn't a disgrace, and her father came in later and told her not to worry. It was better not to be unhappy, her father said: it was better to have courage now.

'Let me tell Doyle to order a car at once.' Mrs Angusthorpe was on her feet, eagerness in her eyes and voice. Her cheeks were flushed from sherry and excitement.

'You're quite outrageous,' said Daphne Jackson.

She left the bar and in the hall Doyle again desired her as she passed. He spoke to her, telling her he'd already ordered a few more bottles of that sherry so that she and Mrs Angusthorpe could sip a little as often as they liked. It was sherry, he repeated, that was very popular in the locality. She nodded and mounted the stairs, not hearing much of what he said, feeling that as she pushed one leg in front of the other her whole body would open and tears would gush from everywhere. Why did she have to put up with talk like that on the first morning of her honeymoon? Why had he casually gone out fishing with his old headmaster? Why had he brought her to this terrible place and then made her drink so that the tension would leave her body? She sobbed on the stairs, causing Doyle to frown and feel concerned for her.

'Are you all right?' Jackson Major asked, standing in the doorway of their room, looking to where she sat, by the window. He closed the door and went to her. 'You've been all right?' he said.

She nodded, smiling a little. She spoke in a low voice: she said she thought it possible that conversations might be heard through the partition wall. She pointed to the wall she spoke of. 'It's only a partition,' she said.

He touched it and agreed, but gave it as his opinion that little could be heard through it since they themselves had not heard the people on the other side of it. Partitions nowadays, he pronounced, were constructed always of soundproof material.

'Let's have a drink before lunch,' she said.

In the hour that had elapsed since she had left Mrs Angusthorpe in the bar she had changed her stockings and her dress. She had washed her face in cold water and had put lipstick and powder on it. She had brushed her suede shoes with a rubber brush.

'All right,' he said. 'We'll have a little drink.'

He kissed her. On the way downstairs he told her about the morning's fishing and the conversations he had had with his old headmaster. Not asking her what she'd like, he ordered both of them gin and tonic in the bar.

'I know her better than you do, sir,' Doyle said, bringing her a glass of sherry, but Jackson Major didn't appear to realize what had happened, being still engrossed in the retailing of the conversations he had had with his old headmaster.

'I want to leave this hotel,' she said. 'At once, darling, after lunch.'

'Daphne – '

'I do.'

She didn't say that Mrs Angusthorpe had urged her to leave him, nor that the Angusthorpes had lain awake during the night, hearing what there was to hear. She simply said she didn't at all like the idea of spending her honeymoon in a hotel which also contained his late headmaster and the headmaster's wife. 'They remember you as a boy,' she said. 'For some reason it makes me edgy. And anyway it's such a nasty hotel.'

She leaned back after that speech, glad that she'd been able to make it as she'd planned to make it. They would move on after lunch, paying whatever

money must necessarily be paid. They would find a
pleasant room in a pleasant hotel and the tension
inside her would gradually relax. In the Hurlingham
Club she had made this tall man look at her when he
spoke to her, she had made him regard her and find
her attractive, as she found him. They had said to one
another that they had fallen in love, he had asked her
to marry him, and she had happily agreed: there was
nothing the matter.

'My dear, it would be quite impossible,' he said.

'Impossible?'

'At this time of year, in the middle of the season?
Hotel rooms are gold dust, my dear. Angusthorpe
was saying as much. His wife's a good sort, you
know – '

'I want to leave here.'

He laughed good-humouredly. He gestured with
his hands, suggesting his helplessness.

'I cannot stay here,' she said.

'You're tired, Daphne.'

'I cannot stay here for a fortnight with the
Angusthorpes. She's a woman who goes on all the
time; there's something the matter with her. While
you go fishing – '

'Darling, I had to go this morning. I felt it polite to
go. If you like, I'll not go out again at all.'

'I've told you what I'd like.'

'Oh, for God's sake!' He turned away from her.
She said:

'I thought you would say yes at once.'

'How the hell can I say yes when we've booked a
room for the next fortnight and we're duty-bound to
pay for it? Do you really think we can just walk up to

that man and say we don't like his hotel and the
people he has staying here?'

'We could make some excuse. We could pretend – '

'Pretend? Pretend, Daphne?'

'Some illness. We could say my mother's ill,' she
hurriedly said. 'Or some aunt who doesn't even exist.
We could hire a car and drive around the coast – '

'Daphne – '

'Why not?'

'For a start, I haven't my driving licence with me.'

'I have.'

'I doubt it, Daphne.'

She thought, and then she agreed that she hadn't.
'We could go to Dublin,' she said with a fresh burst
of urgency. 'Dublin's a lovely place, people say. We
could stay in Dublin and – '

'My dear, this is a tourist country. Millions of
tourists come here every summer. Do you really
believe we'd find decent accommodation in Dublin
in the middle of the season?'

'It wouldn't have to be decent. Some little clean
hotel – '

'Added to which, Daphne, I must honestly tell you
that I have no wish to go gallivanting on my
honeymoon. Nor do I care for the notion of telling
lies about the illness of people who are not ill, or do
not even exist.'

'I'll tell the lies. I'll talk to Mr Doyle directly after
lunch. I'll talk to him now.' She stood up. He shook
his head, reaching for the hand that was nearer to
him.

'What's the matter?' he asked.

Slowly she sat down again.

'Oh, darling,' she said.

'We must be sensible, Daphne. We can't just go gallivanting off – '

'Why do you keep on about gallivanting? What's it matter whether we're gallivanting or not so long as we're enjoying ourselves?'

'Daphne – '

'I'm asking you to do something to please me.'

Jackson Major, about to reply, changed his mind. He smiled at his bride. After a pause, he said:

'If you really want to, Daphne – '

'Well, I do. I think perhaps it'll be awkward here with the Angusthorpes. And it's not what we expected.'

'It's just a question,' said Jackson Major, 'of what we could possibly do. I've asked for my mail to be forwarded here and, as I say, I really believe it would be a case of out of the frying pan into nothing at all. It might prove horribly difficult.'

She closed her eyes and sat for a moment in silence. Then she opened them and, being unable to think of anything else to say, she said:

'I'm sorry.'

He sighed, shrugging his shoulders slightly. He took her hand again. 'You do see, darling?' Before she could reply he added: 'I'm sorry I was angry with you. I didn't mean to be: I'm very sorry.'

He kissed her on the cheek that was near to him. He took her hand. 'Now tell me,' he said, 'about everything that's worrying you.'

She repeated, without more detail, what she had said already, but this time the sentences she spoke did not sound like complaints. He listened to her, sitting back and not interrupting, and then they conversed about all she had said. He agreed that it was a pity about the hotel and explained to her that what had happened, apparently, was that the old proprietor had died during the previous year. It was unfortunate too, he quite agreed, that the Angusthorpes should be here at the same time as they were because it would, of course, have been so much nicer to have been on their own. If she was worried about the partition in their room he would ask that their room should be changed for another one. He hadn't known when she'd mentioned the partition before that it was the Angusthorpes who were on the other side of it. It would be better, really, not to be in the next room to the Angusthorpes since Angusthorpe had once been his headmaster, and he was certain that Doyle would understand a thing like that and agree to change them over, even if it meant greasing Doyle's palm. 'I imagine he'd fall in with anything,' said Jackson Major, 'for a bob or two.'

They finished their drinks and she followed him to the dining-room. There were no thoughts in her mind: no voice, neither her own nor Mrs Angusthorpe's, spoke. For a reason she could not understand and didn't want to bother to understand, the tension within her had snapped and was no longer there. The desire she had felt for tears when she'd walked away from Mrs Angusthorpe was far from her now; she felt a weariness, as though an ordeal was over and she had survived it. She didn't know why she felt like that. All she knew was that he had listened to her: he had been patient and understanding, allowing her to say everything that was in

her mind and then being reassuring. It was not his
fault that the hotel had turned out so unfortunately.
Nor was it his fault that a bullying old man had
sought him out as a fishing companion. He couldn't
help it if his desire for her brought out a clumsiness in
him. He was a man, she thought: he was not the
same as she was: she must meet him half-way. He had
said he was sorry for being angry with her.

In the hall they met the Angusthorpes on their
way to the dining-room also.

'I'm sorry if I upset you,' Mrs Angusthorpe said to
her, touching her arm to hold her back for a
moment. 'I'm afraid my temper ran away with me.'

The two men went ahead, involved in a new
conversation. 'We might try that little tributary this
afternoon,' the headmaster was suggesting.

'I sat there afterwards, seeing how horrid it must
have been for you,' Mrs Angusthorpe said. 'I was
only angry at the prospect of an unpleasant fortnight.
I took it out on you.'

'Don't worry about it.'

'One should keep one's anger to oneself. I feel
embarrassed now,' said Mrs Angusthorpe. 'I'm not
the sort of person – '

'Please don't worry,' murmured Daphne, trying
hard to keep the tiredness that possessed her out of
her voice. She could sleep, she was thinking, for a
week.

'I don't know why I talked like that.'

'You were angry – '

'Yes,' said Mrs Angusthorpe.

She stood still, not looking at Daphne and seeming
not to wish to enter the dining-room. Some people

went by, talking and laughing. Mr Gorman, the solicitor from Dublin, addressed her, but she did not acknowledge his greeting.

'I think we must go in now, Mrs Angusthorpe,' Daphne said.

In her weariness she smiled at Mrs Angusthorpe, suddenly sorry for her because she had so wretched a marriage that it caused her to become emotional with strangers.

'It was just,' said Mrs Angusthorpe, pausing uncertainly in the middle of her sentence and then continuing, 'I felt that perhaps I should say something. I felt, Mrs Jackson – '

'Let's just forget it,' interrupted Daphne, sensing with alarm that Mrs Angusthorpe was about to begin all over again, in spite of her protestations.

'What?'

'I think we must forget it all.'

Daphne smiled again, to reassure the woman who'd been outrageous because her temper had run away with her. She wanted to tell her that just now in the bar she herself had had a small outburst and that in the end she had seen the absurdity of certain suggestions she had made. She wanted to say that her husband had asked her what the matter was and then had said he was sorry. She wanted to explain, presumptuously perhaps, that there must be give and take in marriage, that a bed of roses was something that couldn't be shared. She wanted to say that the tension she'd felt was no longer there, but she couldn't find the energy for saying it.

'Forget it?' said Mrs Angusthorpe. 'Yes, I suppose so. There are things that shouldn't be talked about.'

'It's not that really,' objected Daphne softly. 'It's just that I think you jumped to a lot of wrong conclusions.'

'I had an instinct,' began Mrs Angusthorpe with all her previous eagerness and urgency. 'I saw you at breakfast-time, an innocent girl. I couldn't help remembering.'

'It's different for us,' said Daphne, feeling embarrassed to have to converse again in this intimate vein. 'At heart my husband's patient with me. And understanding too: he listens to me.'

'Of course,' agreed Mrs Angusthorpe, slowly nodding her head and moving at last towards the dining-room.

Broken Homes

'I really think you're marvellous,' the man said.

He was small and plump, with a plump face that had a greyness about it where he shaved; his hair was grey also, falling into a fringe on his forehead. He was untidily dressed, a turtlenecked red jersey beneath a jacket that had a ballpoint pen and a pencil sticking out of the breast pocket. When he stood up his black corduroy trousers developed concertina creases. Nowadays you saw a lot of men like this, Mrs Malby said to herself.

'We're trying to help them,' he said, 'and of course we're trying to help you. The policy is to foster a deeper understanding.' He smiled, displaying small, evenly arranged teeth. 'Between the generations,' he added.

'Well, of course it's very kind,' Mrs Malby said.

He shook his head. He sipped the instant coffee she'd made for him and nibbled the edge of a pink wafer biscuit. As if driven by a compulsion, he dipped the biscuit into the coffee. He said:

'What age actually are you, Mrs Malby?'

'I'm eighty-seven.'

'You really are splendid for eighty-seven.'

He went on talking. He said he hoped he'd be as good himself at eighty-seven. He hoped he'd even be in the land of the living. 'Which I doubt,' he said with a laugh. 'Knowing me.'

Mrs Malby didn't know what he meant by that. She was sure she'd heard him quite correctly, but she could recall nothing he'd previously stated which indicated ill-health. She thought carefully while he continued to sip at his coffee and attend to the mush of biscuit. What he had said suggested that a knowledge of him would cause you to doubt that he'd live to old age. Had he already supplied further knowledge of himself which, due to her slight deafness, she had not heard? If he hadn't, why had he left everything hanging in the air like that? It was difficult to know how best to react, whether to smile or to display concern.

'So what I thought,' he said, 'was that we could send the kids on Tuesday. Say start the job Tuesday morning, eh, Mrs Malby?'

'It's extremely kind of you.'

'They're good kids.'

He stood up. He remarked on her two budgerigars and the geraniums on her window-sill. Her sitting-room was as warm as toast, he said; it was freezing outside.

'It's just that I wondered,' she said, having made up her mind to say it, 'if you could possibly have come to the wrong house?'

'Wrong? *Wrong*? You're Mrs Malby, aren't you?' He raised his voice. 'You're Mrs Malby, love?'

'Oh, yes, it's just that my kitchen isn't really in need of decoration.'

He nodded. His head moved slowly and when it stopped his dark eyes stared at her from beneath his grey fringe. He said, quite softly, what she'd dreaded he might say: that she hadn't understood.

'I'm thinking of the community, Mrs Malby. I'm thinking of you here on your own above a green-

grocer's shop with your two budgies. You can
benefit my kids, Mrs Malby; they can benefit
you. There's no charge of any kind whatsoever.
Put it like this, Mrs Malby: it's an experiment in
community relations.' He paused. He reminded her
of a picture there'd been in a history book, a long
time ago, History with Miss Deacon, a picture of a
Roundhead. 'So you see, Mrs Malby,' he said,
having said something else while he was reminding
her of a Roundhead.

'It's just that my kitchen is really quite nice.'

'Let's have a little look, shall we?'

She led the way. He glanced at the kitchen's
shell-pink walls, and at the white paintwork. It
would cost her nearly a hundred pounds to have
it done, he said; and then, to her horror, he began
all over again, as if she hadn't heard a thing he'd
been saying. He repeated that he was a teacher,
from the school called the Tite Comprehensive. He
appeared to assume that she wouldn't know the
Tite Comprehensive, but she did: an ugly sprawl of
glass-and-concrete buildings, children swinging
along the pavements, shouting obscenities. The
man repeated what he had said before about these
children: that some of them came from broken
homes. The ones he wished to send to her on
Tuesday morning came from broken homes, which
was no joke for them. He felt, he repeated, that we
all had a special duty where such children were
concerned.

Mrs Malby again agreed that broken homes were
to be deplored. It was just, she explained, that she
was thinking of the cost of decorating a kitchen

which didn't need decorating. Paint and brushes
were expensive, she pointed out.

'Freshen it over for you,' the man said, raising his
voice. 'First thing Tuesday, Mrs Malby.'

He went away, and she realized that he hadn't told
her his name. Thinking she might be wrong about
that, she went over their encounter in her mind,
going back to the moment when her doorbell had
sounded. 'I'm from Tite Comprehensive,' was what
he'd said. No name had been mentioned, of that she
was positive.

In her elderliness Mrs Malby liked to be sure of
such details. You had to work quite hard sometimes
at eighty-seven, straining to hear, concentrating
carefully in order to be sure of things. You had to
make it clear you understood because people often
imagined you didn't. Communication was what it
was called nowadays, rather than conversation.

Mrs Malby was wearing a blue dress with a
pattern of darker blue flowers on it. She was a
woman who had been tall but had shrunk a little
with age and had become slightly bent. Scant white
hair crowned a face that was touched with elderly
freckling. Large brown eyes, once her most striking
feature, were quieter than they had been, tired
behind spectacles now. Her husband, Ernest, the
owner of the greengrocer's shop over which she
lived, had died five years ago; her two sons, Derek
and Roy, had been killed in the same month – June
1942 – in the same desert retreat.

The greengrocer's shop was unpretentious, in an
unpretentious street in Fulham called Catherine
Street. The people who owned it now, Jewish

people called King, kept an eye on Mrs Malby.
They watched for her coming and going and if
they missed her one day they'd ring her doorbell
to see that she was all right. She had a niece in
Ealing who looked in twice a year, and another
niece in Islington, who was crippled with arthritis.
Once a week Mrs Grove and Mrs Halbert came
round with Meals on Wheels. A social worker,
Miss Tingle, called; and the Reverend Bush called.
Men came to read the meters.

In her elderliness, living where she'd lived since
her marriage in 1920, Mrs Malby was happy. The
tragedy in her life – the death of her sons – was no
longer a nightmare, and the time that had passed
since her husband's death had allowed her to come
to terms with being on her own. All she wished
for was to continue in these same circumstances
until she died, and she did not fear death. She did
not believe she would be reunited with her sons
and her husband, not at least in a specific sense,
but she could not believe, either, that she would
entirely cease to exist the moment she ceased to
breathe. Having thought about death, it seemed
likely to Mrs Malby that after it came she'd dream,
as in sleep. Heaven and hell were surely no more
than flickers of such pleasant dreaming, or flickers
of a nightmare from which there was no waking
release. No loving omnipotent God, in
Mrs Malby's view, doled out punishments and
reward: human conscience, the last survivor, did
that. The idea of a God, which had puzzled
Mrs Malby for most of her life, made sense when
she thought of it in terms like these, when she

forgot about the mystic qualities claimed for a Church and for Jesus Christ. Yet fearful of offending the Reverend Bush, she kept such conclusions to herself when he came to see her.

All Mrs Malby dreaded now was becoming senile and being forced to enter the Sunset Home in Richmond, of which the Reverend Bush and Miss Tingle warmly spoke. The thought of a communal existence, surrounded by other elderly people, with sing-songs and card-games, was anathema to her. All her life she had hated anything that smacked of communal jolliness, refusing even to go on coach trips. She loved the house above the greengrocer's shop. She loved walking down the stairs and out on to the street, nodding at the Kings as she went by the shop, buying birdseed and eggs and fire-lighters, and fresh bread from Bob Skipps, a man of sixty-two whom she'd remembered being born.

The dread of having to leave Catherine Street ordered her life. With all her visitors she was careful, constantly on the lookout for signs in their eyes which might mean they were diagnosing her as senile. It was for this reason that she listened so intently to all that was said to her, that she concentrated, determined to let nothing slip by. It was for this reason that she smiled and endeavoured to appear agreeable and cooperative at all times. She was well aware that it wasn't going to be up to her to state that she was senile, or to argue that she wasn't, when the moment came.

After the teacher from Tite Comprehensive School had left, Mrs Malby continued to worry.

The visit from this grey-haired man had bewildered
her from the start. There was the oddity of his not
giving his name, and then the way he'd placed a
cigarette in his mouth and had taken it out again,
putting it back in the packet. Had he imagined
cigarette smoke would offend her? He could have
asked, but in fact he hadn't even referred to the
cigarette. Nor had he said where he'd heard about
her: he hadn't mentioned the Reverend Bush, for
instance, or Mrs Grove and Mrs Halbert, or Miss
Tingle. He might have been a customer in the
greengrocer's shop, but he hadn't given any indication that that was so. Added to which, and most of
all, there was the consideration that her kitchen
wasn't in the least in need of attention. She went
to look at it again, beginning to wonder if there were
things about it she couldn't see. She went over in her
mind what the man had said about community
relations. It was difficult to resist men like that, you
had to go on repeating yourself and after a while you
had to assess if you were sounding senile or not. There
was also the consideration that the man was trying to
do good, helping children from broken homes.

'Hi,' a boy with long blond hair said to her on the
Tuesday morning. There were two other boys with
him, one with a fuzz of dark curls all round his head,
the other red-haired, a greased shock that hung to his
shoulders. There was a girl as well, thin and beaky-
faced, chewing something. Between them they
carried tins of paint, brushes, cloths, a blue plastic
bucket and a transistor radio. 'We come to do your
kitchen out,' the blond boy said. 'You Mrs Wheeler
then?'

'No, no. I'm Mrs Malby.'

'That's right, Billo,' the girl said. 'Malby.'

'I thought he says Wheeler.'

'Wheeler's the geyser in the paint shop,' the fuzzy-haired boy said.

'Typical Billo,' the girl said.

She let them in, saying it was very kind of them. She led them to the kitchen, remarking on the way that strictly speaking it wasn't in need of decoration, as they could see for themselves. She'd been thinking it over, she added: she wondered if they'd just like to wash the walls down, which was a task she found difficult to do herself?

They'd do whatever she wanted, they said, no problem. They put their paint tins on the table. The red-haired boy turned on the radio. 'Welcome back to Open House', a cheery voice said and then reminded its listeners that it was the voice of Pete Murray. It said that a record was about to be played for someone in Upminster.

'Would you like some coffee?' Mrs Malby suggested above the noise of the transistor.

'Great,' the blond boy said.

They all wore blue jeans with patches on them. The girl had a T-shirt with the words *I Lay Down With Jesus* on it. The others wore T-shirts of different colours, the blond boy's orange, the fuzzy one's light blue, the red-haired one's red. *Hot Jam-roll* a badge on the chest of the blond boy said; *Jaws* and *Bay City Rollers* other badges said.

Mrs Malby made them Nescafé while they listened to the music. They lit cigarettes, leaning about against the electric stove and against the edge of the table and against a wall. They didn't say anything because they were listening. 'That's a load of crap,' the red-haired boy pronounced eventually, and the others agreed. Even so they went on listening. 'Pete Murray's crappy,' the girl said.

Mrs Malby handed them the cups of coffee, drawing their attention to the sugar she'd put out for them on the table, and to the milk. She smiled at the girl. She said again that it was a job she couldn't manage any more, washing walls.

'Get that, Billo?' the fuzzy-haired boy said. 'Washing walls.'

'Who loves ya, baby?' Billo replied.

Mrs Malby closed the kitchen door on them, hoping they wouldn't take too long because the noise of the transistor was so loud. She listened to it for a quarter of an hour and then she decided to go out and do her shopping.

In Bob Skipps' she said that four children from the Tite Comprehensive had arrived in her house and were at present washing her kitchen walls. She said it again to the man in the fish shop and the man was surprised. It suddenly occurred to her that of course they couldn't have done any painting because she hadn't discussed colours with the teacher. She thought it odd that the teacher hadn't mentioned colours and wondered what colour the paint tins contained. It worried her a little that all that hadn't occurred to her before.

'Hi, Mrs Wheeler,' the boy called Billo said to her in her hall. He was standing there combing his hair, looking at himself in the mirror of the hall-stand. Music was coming from upstairs.

There were yellowish smears on the stair-carpet, which upset Mrs Malby very much. There were similar smears on the landing carpet. 'Oh, but please,' Mrs Malby cried, standing in the kitchen doorway. 'Oh, please, no!' she cried.

Yellow emulsion paint partially covered the shell-pink of one wall. Some had spilt from the tin on to the black-and-white vinyl of the floor and had been walked through. The boy with fuzzy hair was standing on a draining board applying the same paint to the ceiling. He was the only person in the kitchen.

He smiled at Mrs Malby, looking down at her. 'Hi, Mrs Wheeler,' he said.

'But I said only to wash them,' she cried.

She felt tired, saying that. The upset of finding the smears on the carpets and of seeing the hideous yellow plastered over the quiet shell-pink had already taken a toll. Her emotional outburst had caused her face and neck to become warm. She felt she'd like to lie down.

'Eh, Mrs Wheeler?' The boy smiled at her again, continuing to slap paint on to the ceiling. A lot of it dripped back on top of him, on to the draining board and on to cups and saucers and cutlery, and on to the floor. 'D'you fancy the colour, Mrs Wheeler?' he asked her.

All the time the transistor continued to blare, a voice inexpertly singing, a tuneless twanging. The boy referred to this sound, pointing at the transistor with his paintbrush, saying it was great. Unsteadily she crossed the kitchen and turned the transistor off. 'Hey, sod it, missus,' the boy protested angrily.

'I said to wash the walls. I didn't even choose that colour.'

The boy, still annoyed because she'd turned off the radio, was gesturing crossly with the brush. There was paint in the fuzz of his hair and on his T-shirt and his face. Every time he moved the brush about paint flew off it. It speckled the windows, and the small dresser, and the electric stove and the taps and the sink.

'Where's the sound gone?' the boy called Billo demanded, coming into the kitchen and going straight to the transistor.

'I didn't want the kitchen painted,' Mrs Malby said again. 'I told you.'

The singing from the transistor recommenced, louder than before. On the draining board the fuzzy-haired boy began to sway, throwing his body and his head about.

'Please stop him painting,' Mrs Malby shouted as shrilly as she could.

'Here,' the boy called Billo said, bundling her out on to the landing and closing the kitchen door. 'Can't hear myself think in there.'

'I don't want it painted.'

'What's that, Mrs Wheeler?'

'My name isn't Wheeler. I don't want my kitchen painted. I told you.'

'Are we in the wrong house? Only we was told – '

'Will you please wash that paint off?'

'If we come to the wrong house – '

'You haven't come to the wrong house. Please tell that boy to wash off the paint he's put on.'

'Did a bloke from the Comp come in to see you, Mrs Wheeler? Fat bloke?'

'Yes, yes, he did.'

'Only he give instructions – '

'Please would you tell that boy?'

'Whatever you say, Mrs Wheeler.'

'And wipe up the paint where it's spilt on the floor. It's been trampled out, all over my carpets.'

'No problem, Mrs Wheeler.'

Not wishing to return to the kitchen herself, she ran the hot tap in the bathroom on to the sponge-cloth she kept for cleaning the bath. She found that if she rubbed hard enough at the paint on the stair-carpet and on the landing carpet it began to disappear. But the rubbing tired her. As she put away the sponge-cloth, Mrs Malby had a feeling of not quite knowing what was what. Everything that had happened in the last few hours felt like a dream; it also had the feeling of plays she had seen on television; the one thing it wasn't like was reality. As she paused in her bathroom, having placed the sponge-cloth on a ledge under the hand-basin, Mrs Malby saw herself standing there, as she often did in a dream: she saw her body hunched within the same blue dress she'd been wearing when the teacher called, and two touches of red in her pale face, and her white hair tidy on her head and her fingers seeming fragile. In a dream anything could happen next: she might suddenly find herself forty years younger, Derek and Roy might be alive. She might be even younger; Dr Ramsey might be telling her she was pregnant. In a television play it would be different: the children who had come to her house might kill her. What she hoped for from reality was that order would be restored in her kitchen, that all the paint would be washed away from her walls as she had wiped it from her carpets, that the misunderstanding would be over. For an instant she saw herself in her kitchen, making tea for the children, saying it didn't matter. She even heard herself adding that in a life as long as hers you became used to everything.

She left the bathroom; the blare of the transistor still persisted. She didn't want to sit in her sitting-room, having to listen to it. She climbed the stairs to her bedroom, imagining the coolness there, and the quietness.

'Hey,' the girl protested when Mrs Malby opened her bedroom door.

'Sod off, you guys,' the boy with the red hair ordered.

They were in her bed. Their clothes were all over the floor. Her two budgerigars were flying about the room. Protruding from sheets and blankets she could see the boy's naked shoulders and the back of his head. The girl poked her face up from under him. She gazed at Mrs Malby. 'It's not them,' she whispered to the boy. 'It's the woman.'

'Hi there, missus.' The boy twisted his head round. From the kitchen, still loudly, came the noise of the transistor.

'Sorry,' the girl said.

'Why are they up here? Why have you let my birds out? You've no right to behave like this.'

'We needed sex,' the girl explained.

The budgerigars were perched on the looking-glass on the dressing-table, beadily surveying the scene.

'They're really great, them budgies,' the boy said.

Mrs Malby stepped through their garments. The budgerigars remained where they were. They fluttered when she seized them but they didn't offer any resistance. She returned with them to the door.

'You had no right,' she began to say to the two in her bed, but her voice had become weak. It quivered into a useless whisper, and once more she thought that what was happening couldn't be happening. She saw herself again, standing unhappily with the budgerigars.

In her sitting-room she wept. She returned the budgerigars to their cage and sat in an armchair by the window that looked out over Catherine Street. She sat in sunshine, feeling its warmth but not, as she might have done, delighting in it. She wept because she had intensely disliked finding the boy and girl in her bed. Images from the bedroom remained vivid in her mind. On the floor the boy's boots were heavy and black, composed of leather that did not shine. The girl's shoes were green, with huge heels and soles. The girl's underclothes were purple, the boy's dirty. There'd been an unpleasant smell of sweat in her bedroom.

Mrs Malby waited, her head beginning to ache. She dried away her tears, wiping at her eyes and cheeks with a handkerchief. In Catherine Street people passed by on bicycles, girls from the polish factory returning home to lunch, men from the brickworks. People came out of the greengrocer's with leeks and cabbages in baskets, some carrying paper bags. Watching these people in Catherine Street made her feel better, even though her headache was becoming worse. She felt more composed, and more in control of herself.

'We're sorry,' the girl said again, suddenly appearing, teetering on her clumsy shoes. 'We didn't think you'd come up to the bedroom.'

She tried to smile at the girl, but found it hard to do so. She nodded instead.

'The others put the birds in,' the girl said. 'Meant to be a joke, that was.'

She nodded again. She couldn't see how it could be a joke to take two budgerigars from their cage, but she didn't say that.

'We're getting on with the painting now,' the girl said. 'Sorry about that.'

She went away and Mrs Malby continued to watch the people in Catherine Street. The girl had made a mistake when she'd said they were getting on with the painting: what she'd meant was that they were getting on with washing it off. The girl had come straight downstairs to say she was sorry; she hadn't been told by the boys in the kitchen that the paint had been applied in error. When they'd gone, Mrs Malby said to herself she'd open her bedroom window wide in order to get rid of the odour of sweat. She'd put clean sheets on her bed.

From the kitchen, above the noise of the transistor, came the clatter of raised voices. There was laughter and a crash, and then louder laughter. Singing began, attaching itself to the singing from the transistor.

She sat for twenty minutes and then she went and knocked on the kitchen door, not wishing to push the door open in case it knocked someone off a chair. There was no reply. She opened the door gingerly.

More yellow paint had been applied. The whole wall around the window was covered with it, and most of the wall behind the sink. Half of the ceiling had it on it; the woodwork that had been white was now a gloss dark blue. All four of the children were working with brushes. A tin of paint had been upset on the floor.

She wept again, standing there watching them, unable to prevent her tears. She felt them running warmly on her cheeks and then becoming cold. It was in this kitchen that she had cried first of all when the two telegrams had come in 1942, believing when the second one arrived that she would never cease to cry. It would have seemed ridiculous at the time, to cry just because her kitchen was all yellow.

They didn't see her standing there. They went on singing, slapping the paintbrushes back and forth. There'd been neat straight lines where the shell-pink met the white of the woodwork, but now the lines were any old how. The boy with the red hair was applying the dark-blue gloss.

Again the feeling that it wasn't happening possessed Mrs Malby. She'd had a dream a week ago, a particularly vivid dream in which the Prime Minister had stated on television that the Germans had been invited to invade England since England couldn't manage to look after herself any more. That dream had been most troublesome because when she'd woken up in the morning she'd thought it was something she'd seen on television, that she'd actually been sitting in her sitting-room the night before listening to the Prime Minister saying that he and the Leader of the Opposition had decided the best for Britain was invasion. After thinking about it, she'd established that of course it hadn't been true; but even so she'd glanced at the headlines of newspapers when she went out shopping.

'How d'you fancy it?' the boy called Billo called out to her, smiling across the kitchen at her, not noticing that she was upset. 'Neat, Mrs Wheeler?'

She didn't answer. She went downstairs and walked out of her hall door, into Catherine Street and into the greengrocer's that had been her husband's. It never closed in the middle of the day; it never had. She waited and Mr King appeared, wiping his mouth. 'Well then, Mrs Malby?' he said.

He was a big man with a well-kept black moustache and Jewish eyes. He didn't smile much because smiling wasn't his way, but he was in no way morose, rather the opposite.

'So what can I do for you?' he said.

She told him. He shook his head and repeatedly frowned as he listened. His expressive eyes widened. He called his wife.

While the three of them hurried along the pavement to Mrs Malby's open hall door it seemed to her that the Kings doubted her. She could feel them thinking that she must have got it all wrong, that she'd somehow imagined all this stuff about yellow paint and pop music on a radio, and her birds flying around her bedroom while two children were lying in her bed. She didn't blame them; she knew exactly how they felt. But when they entered her house the noise from the transistor could at once be heard.

The carpet of the landing was smeared again with the paint. Yellow footprints led to her sitting-room and out again, back to the kitchen.

'You bloody young hooligans,' Mr King shouted at them. He snapped the switch on the transistor. He told them to stop applying the paint immediately. 'What the hell d'you think you're up to?' he demanded furiously.

'We come to paint out the old ma's kitchen,' the boy called Billo explained, unruffled by Mr King's tone. 'We was carrying out instructions, mister.'

'So it was instructions to spill the blooming paint all over the floor? So it was instructions to cover the windows with it and every knife and fork in the place? So it was instructions to frighten the life out of a poor woman by messing about in her bedroom?'

'No one frightens her, mister.'

'You know what I mean, son.'

Mrs Malby returned with Mrs King and sat in the cubbyhole behind the shop, leaving Mr King to do

his best. At three o'clock he arrived back, saying that
the children had gone. He telephoned the school and
after a delay was put in touch with the teacher who'd
been to see Mrs Malby. He made this telephone call
in the shop but Mrs Malby could hear him saying
that what had happened was a disgrace. 'A woman of
eighty-seven,' Mr King protested, 'thrown into a
state of misery. There'll be something to pay on this,
you know.'

There was some further discussion on the
telephone, and then Mr King replaced the receiver. He put his head into the cubbyhole and
announced that the teacher was coming round
immediately to inspect the damage. 'What can I
entice you to?' Mrs Malby heard him asking a
customer, and a woman's voice replied that she
needed tomatoes, a cauliflower, potatoes and
Bramleys. She heard Mr King telling the woman
what had happened, saying that it had wasted two
hours of his time.

She drank the sweet milky tea which Mrs King
had poured her. She tried not to think of the
yellow paint and the dark-blue gloss. She tried not
to remember the scene in the bedroom and the
smell there'd been, and the new marks that had
appeared on her carpets after she'd wiped off the
original ones. She wanted to ask Mr King if these
marks had been washed out before the paint had
had a chance to dry, but she didn't like to ask this
because Mr King had been so kind and it might
seem like pressing him.

'Kids nowadays,' Mrs King said. 'I just don't
know.'

'Birched they should be,' Mr King said, coming into the cubbyhole and picking up a mug of the milky tea. 'I'd birch the bottoms off them.'

Someone arrived in the shop, Mr King hastened from the cubbyhole. 'What can I entice you to, sir?' Mrs Malby heard him politely inquiring and the voice of the teacher who'd been to see her replied. He said who he was and Mr King wasn't polite any more. An experience like that, Mr King declared thunderously, could have killed an eighty-seven-year-old stone dead.

Mrs Malby stood up and Mrs King came promptly forward to place a hand under her elbow. They went into the shop like that. 'Three and a half p,' Mr King was saying to a woman who'd asked the price of oranges. 'The larger ones at four.'

Mr King gave the woman four of the smaller size and accepted her money. He called out to a youth who was passing by on a bicycle, about to start an afternoon paper round. He was a youth who occasionally assisted him on Saturday mornings: Mr King asked him now if he would mind the shop for ten minutes since an emergency had arisen. Just for once, Mr King argued, it wouldn't matter if the evening papers were a little late.

'Well, you can't say they haven't brightened the place up, Mrs Malby,' the teacher said in her kitchen. He regarded her from beneath his grey image. He touched one of the walls with the tip of a finger. He nodded to himself, appearing to be satisfied.

The painting had been completed, the yellow and the dark-blue gloss. Where the colours met

there were untidily jagged lines. All the paint that
had been spilt on the floor had been wiped away,
but the black-and-white vinyl had become dull
and grubby in the process. The paint had also been
wiped from the windows and from other surfaces,
leaving them smeared. The dresser had been wiped
down and was smeary also. The cutlery and the
taps and the cups and saucers had all been washed
or wiped.

'Well, you wouldn't believe it!' Mrs King
exclaimed. She turned to her husband. However
had he managed it all? she asked him. 'You
should have seen the place!' she said to the
teacher.

'It's just the carpets,' Mr King said. He led the
way from the kitchen to the sitting-room, pointing
at the yellow on the landing carpet and on the
sitting-room one. 'The blooming stuff dried,' he
explained, 'before we could get to it. That's where
compensation comes in.' He spoke sternly, addressing the teacher. 'I'd say she has a bob or two
owing.'

Mrs King nudged Mrs Malby, drawing attention
to the fact that Mr King was doing his best for her.
The nudge suggested that all would be well because a
sum of money would be paid, possibly even a larger
sum than was merited. It suggested also that
Mrs Malby in the end might find herself doing
rather well.

'Compensation?' the teacher said, bending down
and scratching at the paint on the sitting-room
carpet. 'I'm afraid compensation's out of the question.'

'She's had her carpets ruined,' Mr King snapped quickly. 'This woman's been put about, you know.'

'She got her kitchen done free,' the teacher snapped back at him.

'They released her pets. They got up to tricks in a bed. You'd no damn right – '

'These kids come from broken homes, sir. I'll do my best with your carpets, Mrs Malby.'

'But what about my kitchen?' she whispered. She cleared her throat because her whispering could hardly be heard. 'My kitchen?' she whispered again.

'What about it, Mrs Malby?'

'I didn't want it painted.'

'Oh, don't be silly now.'

The teacher took his jacket off and threw it impatiently on to a chair. He left the sitting-room. Mrs Malby heard him running a tap in the kitchen.

'It was best to finish the painting, Mrs Malby,' Mr King said. 'Otherwise the kitchen would have driven you mad, half done like that. I stood over them till they finished it.'

'You can't take paint off, dear,' Mrs King said, 'once it's on. You've done wonders, Leo,' she said to her husband. 'Young devils.'

'We'd best be getting back,' Mr King said.

'It's quite nice, you know,' his wife added. 'Your kitchen's quite cheerful, dear.'

The Kings went away and the teacher rubbed at the yellow on the carpets with her washing-up brush. The landing carpet was marked anyway, he pointed out, poking a finger at the stains left behind by the paint she'd removed herself with the sponge-cloth from the bathroom. She must be delighted with the kitchen, he said.

She knew she mustn't speak. She'd known she mustn't when the Kings had been there; she knew she mustn't now. She might have reminded the Kings that she'd chosen the original colours in the kitchen herself. She might have complained to the man as he rubbed at her carpets that the carpets would never be the same again. She watched him, not saying anything, not wishing to be regarded as a nuisance. The Kings would have considered her a nuisance too, agreeing to let children into her kitchen to paint it and then making a fuss. If she became a nuisance the teacher and the Kings would drift on to the same side, and the Reverend Bush would somehow be on that side also, and Miss Tingle, and even Mrs Grove and Mrs Halbert. They would agree among themselves that what had happened had to do with her elderliness, with her not understanding that children who brought paint into a kitchen were naturally going to use it.

'I defy anyone to notice that,' the teacher said, standing up, gesturing at the yellow blurs that remained on her carpets. He put his jacket on. He left the washing-up brush and the bowl of water he'd been using on the floor of her sitting-room. 'All's well that ends well,' he said. 'Thanks for your cooperation, Mrs Malby.'

She thought of her two sons, Derek and Roy, not knowing quite why she thought of them now. She descended the stairs with the teacher, who was

cheerfully talking about community relations. You
had to make allowances, he said, for kids like that;
you had to try and understand; you couldn't just
walk away.

Quite suddenly she wanted to tell him about
Derek and Roy. In the desire to talk about them
she imagined their bodies, as she used to in the past,
soon after they'd been killed. They lay on desert
sand, desert birds swooped down on them. Their
four eyes were gone. She wanted to explain to the
teacher that they'd been happy, a contented family in
Catherine Street, until the war came and smashed
everything to pieces. Nothing had been the same
afterwards. It hadn't been easy to continue with
nothing to continue for. Each room in the house
had contained different memories of the two boys
growing up. Cooking and cleaning had seemed
pointless. The shop which would have been theirs
would have to pass to someone else.

And yet time had soothed the awful double
wound. The horror of the emptiness had been lived
with, and if having the Kings in the shop now wasn't
the same as having your sons there at least the Kings
were kind. Thirty-four years after the destruction of
your family you were happy in your elderliness
because time had been merciful. She wanted to tell
the teacher that also, she didn't know why, except
that in some way it seemed relevant. But she didn't
tell him because it would have been difficult to
begin, because in the effort there'd be the danger
of seeming senile. Instead she said goodbye, concentrating on that. She said she was sorry, saying it just to
show she was aware that she hadn't made herself clear

to the children. Conversation had broken down between the children and herself, she wanted him to know she knew it had.

He nodded vaguely, not listening to her. He was trying to make the world a better place, he said. 'For kids like that, Mrs Malby. Victims of broken homes.'

A Meeting in Middle Age

'I am Mrs da Tanka,' said Mrs da Tanka. 'Are you Mr Mileson?'

The man nodded, and they walked together the length of the platform, seeking a compartment that might offer them a welcome, or failing that, and they knew the more likely, simple privacy. They carried each a small suitcase, Mrs da Tanka's of white leather or some material manufactured to resemble it, Mr Mileson's battered and black. They did not speak as they marched purposefully: they were strangers one to another, and in the noise and the bustle, examining the lighted windows of the carriages, there was little that might constructively be said.

'A ninety-nine years' lease,' Mr Mileson's father had said, 'taken out in 1862 by my grandfather, whom of course you never knew. Expiring in your lifetime, I fear. Yet you will by then be in a sound position to accept the misfortune. To renew what has come to an end; to keep the property in the family.' The property was an expression that glorified. The house was small and useful, one of a row, one of a kind easily found; but the lease when the time came was not renewable – which released Mr Mileson of a problem. Bachelor, childless, the end of the line, what use was a house to him for a further ninety-nine years?

Mrs da Tanka, sitting opposite him, drew a magazine from an assortment she carried. Then, checking herself, said: 'We could talk. Or do you prefer to conduct the business in silence?' She was a woman who filled, but did not overflow from, a fair-sized, elegant, quite expensive tweed suit. Her hair, which was grey, did not appear so; it was tightly held to her head, a reddish-gold colour. Born into another class she would have been a chirpy woman; she guarded against her chirpiness, she disliked the quality in her. There was often laughter in her eyes, and as often as she felt it there she killed it by the severity of her manner.

'You must not feel embarrassment,' Mrs da Tanka said. 'We are beyond the age of giving in to awkwardness in a situation. You surely agree?'

Mr Mileson did not know. He did not know how or what he should feel. Analysing his feelings he could come to no conclusion. He supposed he was excited but it was more difficult than it seemed to track down the emotions. He was unable, therefore, to answer Mrs da Tanka. So he just smiled.

Mrs da Tanka, who had once been Mrs Horace Spire and was not likely to forget it, considered those days. It was a logical thing for her to do, for they were days that had come to an end as these present days were coming to an end. Termination was on her mind: to escape from Mrs da Tanka into Mrs Spire was a way of softening the worry that was with her now, and a way of seeing it in proportion to a lifetime.

'If that is what you want,' Horace had said, 'then by all means have it. Who shall do the dirty work –

you or I?' This was his reply to her request for a divorce. In fact, at the time of speaking, the dirty work as he called it was already done: by both of them.

'It is a shock for me,' Horace had continued. 'I thought we could jangle along for many a day. Are you seriously involved elsewhere?'

In fact she was not, but finding herself involved at all reflected the inadequacy of her married life and revealed a vacuum that once had been love.

'We are better apart,' she had said. 'It is bad to get used to the habit of being together. We must take our chances while we may, while there is still time.'

In the railway carriage she recalled the conversation with vividness, especially that last sentence, most especially the last five words of it. The chance she had taken was da Tanka, eight years ago. 'My God,' she said aloud, 'what a pompous bastard he turned out to be.'

Mr Mileson had a couple of those weekly publications for which there is no accurate term in the language: a touch of a single colour on the front – floppy, half-intellectual things, somewhere between a journal and a magazine. While she had her honest mags. *Harper's. Vogue.* Shiny and smart and rather silly. Or so thought Mr Mileson. He had opened them at dentists' and doctors', leafed his way through the ridiculous advertisements and aptly titled model girls, unreal girls in unreal poses, devoid it seemed of sex, and half the time of life. So that was the kind of woman she was.

'Who?' said Mr Mileson.

'Oh, who else, good heavens! Da Tanka I mean.'

Eight years of da Tanka's broad back, so fat it might have been padded beneath the skin. He had often presented it to her.

'I shall be telling you about da Tanka,' she said. 'There are interesting facets to the man; though God knows, he is scarcely interesting in himself.'

It was a worry, in any case, owning a house. Seeing to the roof; noticing the paint cracking on the outside, and thinking about damp in mysterious places. Better off he was, in the room in Swiss Cottage; cosier in winter. They'd pulled down the old house by now, with all the others in the road. Flats were there instead: bulking up to the sky, with a million or so windows. All the gardens were gone, all the gnomes and the Snow White dwarfs, all the winter bulbs and the little paths of crazy paving; the bird-baths and bird-boxes and bird-tables; the mini-ature sandpits, and the metal edging, ornate, for flower-beds.

'We must move with the times,' said Mrs da Tanka, and he realized that he had been speaking to her; or speaking aloud and projecting the remarks in her direction since she was there.

His mother had made the rockery. Aubrietia and sarsaparilla and pinks and Christmas roses. Her brother, his uncle Edward, bearded and queer, brought seaside stones in his motor-car. His father had shrugged his distaste for the project, as indeed for all projects of this nature, seeing the removal of stones from the seashore as being in some way disgraceful, even dishonest. Behind the rockery there were loganberries: thick, coarse, inedible fruit, never fully ripe. But nobody, certainly not Mr Mileson, had had the heart to pull away the bushes.

'Weeks would pass,' said Mrs da Tanka, 'without the exchange of a single significant sentence. We lived in the same house, ate the same meals, drove out in the same car, and all he would ever say was: "It is time the central heating was on." Or: "These windscreen-wipers aren't working."'

Mr Mileson didn't know whether she was talking about Mr da Tanka or Mr Spire. They seemed like the same man to him: shadowy, silent fellows who over the years had shared this woman with the well-tended hands.

'He will be wearing city clothes,' her friend had said, 'grey or non-descript. He is like anyone else except for his hat, which is big and black and eccentric.' An odd thing about him, the hat: like a wild oat almost.

There he had been, by the tobacco kiosk, punctual and expectant; gaunt of face, thin, fiftyish; with the old-fashioned hat and the weekly papers that somehow matched it, but did not match him.

'Now would you blame me, Mr Mileson? Would you blame me for seeking freedom from such a man?'

The hat lay now on the luggage-rack with his carefully folded overcoat. A lot of his head was bald, whitish and tender like good dripping. His eyes were sad, like those of a retriever puppy she had known in her childhood. Men are often like dogs, she thought; women more akin to cats. The train moved smoothly, with rhythm, through the night. She thought of da Tanka and Horace Spire, wondering where Spire was now. Opposite her, he thought about the ninety-nine-year lease and the two plates, one from last night's supper, the other from breakfast, that he had left unwashed in the room at Swiss Cottage.

'This seems your kind of place,' Mr Mileson said, surveying the hotel from its ornate hall.

'Gin and lemon, gin and lemon,' said Mrs da Tanka, matching the words with action: striding to the bar.

Mr Mileson had rum, feeling it a more suitable drink, though he could not think why. 'My father drank rum with milk in it. An odd concoction.'

'Frightful, it sounds. Da Tanka is a whisky man. My previous liked stout. Well, well, so here we are.'

Mr Mileson looked at her. 'Dinner is next on the agenda.'

But Mrs da Tanka was not to be moved. They sat while she drank many measures of the drink; and when they rose to demand dinner they discovered that the restaurant was closed and were ushered to a grill-room.

'You organized that badly, Mr Mileson.'

'I organized nothing. I know the rules of these places. I repeated them to you. You gave me no chance to organize.'

'A chop and an egg or something. Da Tanka at least could have got us soup.'

In 1931 Mr Mileson had committed fornication with the maid in his parents' house. It was the only occasion, and he was glad that adultery was not expected of him with Mrs da Tanka. In it she would

be more experienced than he, and he did not relish
the implication. The grill-room was lush and vulgar.
'This seems your kind of place,' Mr Mileson repeated
rudely.

'At least it is warm. And the lights don't glare.
Why not order some wine?'

Her husband must remain innocent. He was a
person of importance, in the public eye. Mr Mileson's
friend had repeated it, the friend who knew Mrs da
Tanka's solicitor. All expenses paid, the friend had
said, and a little fee as well. Nowadays Mr Mileson
could do with little fees. And though at the time he
had rejected the suggestion downright, he had later
seen that friend – acquaintance really – in the pub he
went to at half past twelve on Sundays, and had
agreed to take part in the drama. It wasn't just the
little fee; there was something rather like prestige in
the thing; his name as co-respondent – now *there* was
something you'd never have guessed! The hotel bill
to find its way to Mrs da Tanka's husband, who
would pass it to his solicitor. Breakfast in bed, and
remember the face of the maid who brought it. Pass
the time of day with her, and make sure she
remembered yours. Oh very nice, the man in the
pub said, very nice Mrs da Tanka was – or so he was
led to believe. He batted his eyes at Mr Mileson; but
Mr Mileson said it didn't matter, surely, about Mrs da
Tanka's niceness. He knew his duties: there was
nothing personal about them. He'd do it himself,
the man in the pub explained, only he'd never be
able to keep his hands off an attractive middle-aged
woman. That was the trouble about finding someone
for the job.

'I've had a hard life,' Mrs da Tanka confided. 'Tonight I need your sympathy, Mr Mileson. Tell me I have your sympathy.' Her face and neck had reddened: chirpiness was breaking through.

In the house, in a cupboard beneath the stairs, he had kept his gardening boots. Big, heavy army boots, once his father's. He had worn them at weekends, poking about in the garden.

'The lease came to an end two years ago,' he told Mrs da Tanka. 'There I was with all that stuff, all my gardening tools, and the furniture and bric-à-brac of three generations to dispose of. I can tell you it wasn't easy to know what to throw away.'

'Mr Mileson, I don't like that waiter.'

Mr Mileson cut his steak with care: a three-cornered piece, neat and succulent. He loaded mushroom and mustard on it, added a sliver of potato and carried the lot to his mouth. He masticated and drank some wine.

'Do you know the waiter?'

Mrs da Tanka laughed unpleasantly; like ice cracking. 'Why should I know the waiter? I do not generally know waiters. Do *you* know the waiter?'

'I ask because you claim to dislike him.'

'May I not dislike him without an intimate knowledge of the man?'

'You may do as you please. It struck me as a premature decision, that is all.'

'What decision? What is premature? What are you talking about? Are you drunk?'

'The decision to dislike the waiter I thought to be premature. I do not know about being drunk. Probably I am a little. One has to keep one's spirits up.'

'Have you ever thought of wearing an eye-patch, Mr Mileson? I think it would suit you. You need distinction. Have you led an empty life? You give the impression of an empty life.'

'My life has been as many other lives. Empty of some things, full of others. I am in possession of all my sight, though. My eyes are real. Neither is a pretence. I see no call for an eye-patch.'

'It strikes me you see no call for anything. You have never lived, Mr Mileson.'

'I do not understand that.'

'Order us more wine.'

Mr Mileson indicated with his hand and the waiter approached. 'Some other waiter, please,' Mrs da Tanka cried. 'May we be served by another waiter?'

'Madam?' said the waiter.

'We do not take to you. Will you send another man to our table?'

'I am the only waiter on duty, madam.'

'It's quite all right,' said Mr Mileson.

'It's not quite all right. I will not have this man at our table, opening and dispensing wine.'

'Then we must go without.'

'I am the only waiter on duty, madam.'

'There are other employees of the hotel. Send us a porter or the girl at the reception.'

'It is not their duty, madam – '

'Oh nonsense, nonsense. Bring us the wine, man, and have no more to-do.'

Unruffled, the waiter moved away. Mrs da Tanka hummed a popular tune.

'Are you married, Mr Mileson? Have you in the past been married?'

'No, never married.'

'I have been married twice. I am married now. I am throwing the dice for the last time. God knows how I shall find myself. You are helping to shape my destiny. What a fuss that waiter made about the wine!'

'That is a little unfair. It was you, you know – '

'Behave like a gentleman, can't you? Be on my side since you are with me. Why must you turn on me? Have I harmed you?'

'No, no. I was merely establishing the truth.'

'Here is the man again with the wine. He is like a bird. Do you think he has wings strapped down beneath his waiter's clothes? You are like a bird,' she repeated, examining the waiter's face. 'Has some fowl played a part in your ancestry?'

'I think not, madam.'

'Though you cannot be sure. How can you be sure? How can you say you think not when you know nothing about it?'

The waiter poured the wine in silence. He was not embarrassed, Mr Mileson noted; not even angry.

'Bring coffee,' Mrs da Tanka said.

'Madam.'

'How servile waiters are! How I hate servility, Mr Mileson! I could not marry a servile man. I could not marry that waiter, not for all the tea in China.'

'I did not imagine you could. The waiter does not seem your sort.'

'He is your sort. You like him, I think. Shall I leave you to converse with him?'

'Really! What would I say to him? I know nothing about the waiter except what he is in a professional sense. I do not wish to know. It is not my habit to go about consorting with waiters after they have waited on me.'

'I am not to know that. I am not to know what your sort is, or what your personal and private habits are. How could I know? We have only just met.'

'You are clouding the issue.'

'You are as pompous as da Tanka. Da Tanka would say issue and clouding.'

'What your husband would say is no concern of mine.'

'You are meant to be my lover, Mr Mileson. Can't you act it a bit? My husband must concern you dearly. You must wish to tear him limb from limb. Do you wish it?'

'I have never met the man. I know nothing of him.'

'Well then, pretend. Pretend for the waiter's sake. Say something violent in the waiter's hearing. Break an oath. Blaspheme. Bang your fist on the table.'

'I was not told I should have to behave like that. It is against my nature.'

'What is your nature?'

'I'm shy and self-effacing.'

'You are an enemy to me. I don't understand your sort. You have not got on in the world. You take on commissions like this. Where is your self-respect?'

'Elsewhere in my character.'

'You have no personality.'

'That is a cliché. It means nothing.'

'Sweet nothings for lovers, Mr Mileson! Remember that.'

They left the grill-room and mounted the stairs in silence. In their bedroom Mrs da Tanka unpacked a dressing-gown. 'I shall undress in the bathroom. I shall be absent a matter of ten minutes.'

Mr Mileson slipped from his clothes into pyjamas. He brushed his teeth at the wash-basin, cleaned his nails and splashed a little water on his face. When Mrs da Tanka returned he was in bed.

To Mr Mileson she seemed a trifle bigger without her daytime clothes. He remembered corsets and other containing garments. He did not remark upon it.

Mrs da Tanka turned out the light and they lay without touching between the cold sheets of the double bed.

He would leave little behind, he thought. He would die and there would be the things in the room, rather a number of useless things with sentimental value only. Ornaments and ferns. Reproductions of paintings. A set of eggs, birds' eggs he had collected as a boy. They would pile all the junk together and probably try to burn it. Then perhaps they would light a couple of those fumigating candles in the room, because people are insulting when other people die.

'Why did you not get married?' Mrs da Tanka said.

'Because I do not greatly care for women.' He said it, throwing caution to the winds, waiting for her attack.

'Are you a homosexual?'

The word shocked him. 'Of course I'm not.'

'I only asked. They go in for this kind of thing.'

'That does not make me one.'

'I often thought Horace Spire was more that way than any other. For all the attention he paid to me.'

As a child she had lived in Shropshire. In those days
she loved the country, though without knowing, or
wishing to know, the names of flowers or plants or
trees. People said she looked like Alice in Wonderland.

'Have you ever been to Shropshire, Mr Mileson?'

'No. I am very much a Londoner. I lived in the
same house all my life. Now the house is no longer
there. Flats replace it. I live in Swiss Cottage.'

'I thought you might. I thought you might live in
Swiss Cottage.'

'Now and again I miss the garden. As a child I
collected birds' eggs on the common. I have kept
them all these years.'

She had kept nothing. She cut the past off every so
often, remembering it when she cared to, without
the aid of physical evidence.

'The hard facts of life have taken their toll of me,'
said Mrs da Tanka. 'I met them first at twenty. They
have been my companions since.'

'It was a hard fact the lease coming to an end. It
was hard to take at the time. I did not accept it until it
was well upon me. Only the spring before I had
planted new delphiniums.'

'My father told me to marry a good man. To be
happy and have children. Then he died. I did none of
those things. I do not know why except that I did
not care to. Then old Horry Spire put his arm around
me and there we were. Life is as you make it, I
suppose. I was thinking of homosexual in relation to
that waiter you were interested in downstairs.'

'I was not interested in the waiter. He was hard
done by, by you, I thought. There was no more to it
than that.'

Mrs da Tanka smoked and Mr Mileson was nervous; about the situation in general, about the glow of the cigarette in the darkness. What if the woman dropped off to sleep? He had heard of fires started by careless smoking. What if in her confusion she crushed the cigarette against some part of his body? Sleep was impossible: one cannot sleep with the thought of waking up in a furnace, with the bells of fire brigades clanging a death knell.

'I will not sleep tonight,' said Mrs da Tanka, a statement which frightened Mr Mileson further. For all the dark hours the awful woman would be there, twitching and puffing beside him. *I am mad. I am out of my mind to have brought this upon myself.* He heard the words. He saw them on paper, written in his handwriting. He saw them typed, and repeated again as on a telegram. The letters jolted and lost their order. The words were confused, skulking behind a fog. 'I am mad,' Mr Mileson said, to establish the thought completely, to bring it into the open. It was a habit of his; for a moment he had forgotten the reason for the thought, thinking himself alone.

'Are you telling me now you are mad?' asked Mrs da Tanka, alarmed. 'Gracious, are you worse than a homo? Are you some sexual pervert? Is that what you are doing here? Certainly that was not my plan, I do assure you. You have nothing to gain from me, Mr Mileson. If there is trouble I shall ring the bell.'

'I am mad to be here. I am mad to have agreed to all this. What came over me I do not know. I have only just realized the folly of the thing.'

'Arise then, dear Mileson, and break your agreement, your promise and your undertaking. You are
an adult man, you may dress and walk from the
room.'

They were all the same, she concluded: except that
while others had some passing superficial recommen-
dation, this one it seemed had none. There was
something that made her sick about the thought of
the stringy limbs that were stretched out beside her.
What lengths a woman will go to to rid herself of a
horror like da Tanka!

He had imagined it would be a simple thing. It had
sounded like a simple thing: a good thing rather than a
bad one. A good turn for a lady in need. That was as he
had seen it. With the little fee already in his possession.

Mrs da Tanka lit another cigarette and threw the
match on the floor.

'What kind of a life have you had? You had not
the nerve for marriage. Nor the brains for success.
The truth is you might not have lived.' She laughed
in the darkness, determined to hurt him as he had
hurt her in his implication that being with her was an
act of madness.

Mr Mileson had not before done a thing like this.
Never before had he not weighed the pros and cons
and seen that danger was absent from an undertaking.
The thought of it all made him sweat. He saw in the
future further deeds: worse deeds, crimes and irre-
sponsibilities.

Mrs da Tanka laughed again. But she was thinking
of something else.

'You have never slept with a woman, is that it?
Ah, you poor thing! What a lot you have not had the

courage for!' The bed heaved with the raucous noise that was her laughter, and the bright spark of her cigarette bobbed about in the air.

She laughed, quietly now and silently, hating him as she hated da Tanka and had hated Horace Spire. Why could he not be some young man, beautiful and nicely mannered and gay? Surely a young man would have come with her? Surely there was one amongst all the millions who would have done the chore with relish, or at least with charm?

'You are as God made you,' said Mr Mileson. 'You cannot help your shortcomings, though one would think you might by now have recognized them. To others you may be all sorts of things. To me you are a frightful woman.'

'Would you not stretch out a hand to the frightful woman? Is there no temptation for the woman's flesh? Are you a eunuch, Mr Mileson?'

'I have had the women I wanted. I am doing you a favour. Hearing of your predicament and pressed to help you, I agreed in a moment of generosity. Stranger though you were I did not say no.'

'That does not make you a gentleman.'

'And I do not claim it does. I am gentleman enough without it.'

'You are nothing without it. This is your sole experience. In all your clerkly subservience you have not paused to live. You know I am right, and as for being a gentleman − well, you are of the lower middle classes. There has never been an English gentleman born of the lower middle classes.'

She was trying to remember what she looked like; what her face was like, how the wrinkles were spread, how old she looked and what she might pass for in a crowd. Would men not be cagey now and think that she must be difficult in her ways to have parted twice from husbands? Was there a third time coming up? Third time lucky, she thought. Who would have her, though, except some loveless Mileson?

'You have had no better life than I,' said Mr Mileson. 'You are no more happy now. You have failed, and it is cruel to laugh at you.'

They talked and the hatred grew between them.

'In my childhood young men flocked about me, at dances in Shropshire that my father gave to celebrate my beauty. Had the fashion been duels, duels there would have been. Men killed or maimed for life, carrying a lock of my hair on their breast.'

'You are a creature now, with your face and your fingernails. Mutton dressed as lamb, Mrs da Tanka!'

Beyond the curtained windows the light of dawn broke into the night. A glimpse of it crept into the room, noticed and welcomed by its occupants.

'You should write your memoirs, Mr Mileson. To have seen the changes in your time and never to know a thing about them! You are like an occasional table. Or a coat-rack in the hall of a boarding-house. Who shall mourn at your grave, Mr Mileson?'

He felt her eyes upon him; and the mockery of the words sank into his heart with intended precision. He turned to her and touched her, his hands groping about her shoulders. He had meant to grasp her neck, to feel the muscles struggle beneath his fingers, to terrify the life out of her. But she, thinking the gesture was the beginning of an embrace, pushed

him away, swearing at him and laughing. Surprised
by the misunderstanding, he left her alone.

The train was slow. The stations crawled by, similar
and ugly. She fixed her glance on him, her eyes
sharpened; cold and powerful.

She had won the battle, though technically the
victory was his. Long before the time arranged for
their breakfast Mr Mileson had leaped from bed. He
dressed and breakfasted alone in the dining-room.
Shortly afterwards, after sending to the bedroom for
his suitcase, he left the hotel, informing the receptionist that the lady would pay the bill. Which in
time she had done, and afterwards pursued him to the
train, where now, to disconcert him, she sat in the
facing seat of an empty compartment.

'Well,' said Mrs da Tanka, 'you have shot your
bolt. You have taken the only miserable action you
could. You have put the frightful woman in her
place. Have we a right,' she added, 'to expect
anything better of the English lower classes?'

Mr Mileson had foolishly left his weekly magazines
and the daily paper at the hotel. He was obliged to sit
bare-faced before her, pretending to observe the
drifting landscape. In spite of everything, guilt
gnawed him a bit. When he was back in his room
he would borrow the vacuum cleaner and give it a
good going over: the exercise would calm him. A
glass of beer in the pub before lunch; lunch in the
ABC; perhaps an afternoon cinema. It was Saturday
today: this, more or less, was how he usually spent
Saturday. Probably from lack of sleep he would doze
off in the cinema. People would nudge him to draw

attention to his snoring; that had happened before, and was not pleasant.

'To give you birth,' she said, 'your mother had long hours of pain. Have you thought of that, Mr Mileson? Have you thoughts of that poor woman crying out, clenching her hands and twisting the sheets? Was it worth it, Mr Mileson? You tell me now, was it worth it?'

He could leave the compartment and sit with other people. But that would be too great a satisfaction for Mrs da Tanka. She would laugh loudly at his going, might even pursue him to mock in public.

'What you say about me, Mrs da Tanka, can equally be said of you.'

'Are we two peas in a pod? It's an explosive pod in that case.'

'I did not imply that. I would not wish to find myself sharing a pod with you.'

'Yet you shared a bed. And were not man enough to stick to your word. You are a worthless coward, Mr Mileson. I expect you know it.'

'I know myself, which is more than can be said in your case. Do you not think occasionally to see yourself as others see you? An ageing woman, faded and ugly, dubious in morals and personal habits. What misery you must have caused those husbands!'

'They married me, and got good value. You know that, yet dare not admit it.'

'I will scarcely lose sleep worrying the matter out.'

It was a cold morning, sunny with a clear sky. Passengers stepping from the train at the intermediate stations muffled up against the temperature, finding it too much after the warm fug within. Women with baskets. Youths. Men with children, with dogs collected from the guard's van.

Da Tanka, she had heard, was living with another woman. Yet he refused to admit being the guilty party. It would not do for someone like da Tanka to be a public adulterer. So he had said. Pompously. Crossly. Horace Spire, to give him his due, hadn't given a damn one way or the other.

'When you die, Mr Mileson, have you a preference for the flowers on your coffin? It is a question I ask because I might send you off a wreath. That lonely wreath. From ugly, frightful Mrs da Tanka.'

'What?' said Mr Mileson, and she repeated the question.

'Oh well – cow-parsley, I suppose.' He said it, taken off his guard by the image she created; because it was an image he often saw and thought about. Hearse and coffin and he within. It would not be like that probably. Anticipation was not in Mr Mileson's life. Remembering, looking back, considering events and emotions that had been at the time mundane perhaps – this kind of thing was more to his liking. For by hindsight there was pleasure in the stream of time. He could not establish his funeral in his mind; he tried often but ended up always with a funeral he had known: a repetition of his parents' passing and the accompanying convention.

'Cow-parsley?' said Mrs da Tanka. Why did the man say cow-parsley? Why not roses or lilies or something in a pot? There had been cow-parsley in Shropshire; cow-parsley on the verges of dusty lanes; cow-parsley in hot fields buzzing with bees; great white swards rolling down to the river. She

had sat among it on a picnic with dolls. She had
lain on it, laughing at the beautiful anaemic blue of
the sky. She had walked through it by night,
loving it.

'Why did you say cow-parsley?'

He did not know, except that once on a rare
family outing to the country he had seen it and
remembered it. Yet in his garden he had grown
delphiniums and wallflowers and asters and sweet-
peas.

She could smell it again: a smell that was almost
nothing: fields and the heat of the sun on her face,
laziness and summer. There was a red door somewhere, faded and blistered, and she sat against it,
crouched on a warm step, a child dressed in the
fashion of the time.

'Why did you say cow-parsley?'

He remembered, that day, asking the name of the
white powdery growth. He had picked some and
carried it home; and had often since thought of it,
though he had not come across a field of cow-parsley
for years.

She tried to speak again, but after the night there
were no words she could find that would fit. The
silence stuck between them, and Mr Mileson knew
by instinct all that it contained. She saw an image of
herself and him, strolling together from the hotel, in
this same sunshine, at this very moment, lingering on
the pavement to decide their direction and agreeing
to walk to the promenade. She mouthed and
grimaced and the sweat broke on her body, and
she looked at him once and saw words die on his lips,
lost in his suspicion of her.

The train stopped for the last time. Doors banged; the throng of people passed them by on the platform outside. They collected their belongings and left the train together. A porter, interested in her legs, watched them walk down the platform. They passed through the barrier and parted, moving in their particular directions. She to her new flat where milk and mail, she hoped, awaited her. He to his room; to the two unwashed plates on the draining board and the forks with egg on the prongs; and the little fee propped up on the mantelpiece, a pink cheque for five pounds, peeping out from behind a china cat.

Widows

Waking on a warm, bright morning in early October, Catherine found herself a widow. In some moment during the night Matthew had gone peacefully: had there been pain or distress she would have known it. Yet what lay beside her in the bed was less than a photograph now, the fallen jaw harshly distorting a face she'd loved.

Tears ran on Catherine's cheeks and dripped on to her nightdress. She knelt by the bedside, then drew the sheet over the still features. Quiet, gently spoken, given to thought before offering an opinion, her husband had been regarded by Catherine as cleverer and wiser than she was herself, and more charitable in his view of other people. In his business life – the sale of agricultural machinery – he had been known as a man of his word. For miles around, far beyond the town and its immediate neighbourhood, the farm people who had been his customers repaid his honesty and straight dealing with respect. At Christmas there had been gifts of fowls and fish, jars of cream, sacks of potatoes. The funeral would be well attended. 'There'll be a comfort in the memories, Catherine,' Matthew had said more than once, attempting to anticipate the melancholy of their separation; they had known that it was soon to be.

He would have held the memories to him if he'd been the one remaining. 'Whichever is left,' he reminded Catherine as they grew old, 'it's only for the time being.' And in that time being one or other of them would manage in what had previously been the other's domain: he working the washing machine, ironing his sheets and trousers, cooking as he had watched her cook, using the Electrolux; she arranging for someone to undertake the small repairs he had attended to in the house if she or her sister couldn't manage them, paying the household bills and keeping an eye on the bank balance. Matthew had never minded talking about their separation, and had taught her not to mind either.

On her knees by the bedside Catherine prayed, then her tears came again. She reached out for his hand and grasped the cold, stiff fingers beneath the bedclothes. 'Oh, love,' she whispered. 'Oh, love.'

The three sons of the marriage came for the funeral, remaining briefly, with their families, in the town where they had spent their childhood. Father Cahill intoned the last words in the cemetery, and soon after that Catherine and her sister Alicia were alone in the house again. Alicia had lived there since her own husband's death, nine years ago; she was the older of the two sisters – fifty-seven, almost fifty-eight.

The house that for Catherine was still haunted by her husband's recent presence was comfortable, with a narrow hall and a kitchen at the back, and bedrooms on two floors. Outside, it was colour-washed blue, with white window frames and hall door – the last house of the town, the first on the Dublin road. Opposite was the convent school, behind silver-painted railings, three sides enclosed

by the drab concrete of its classrooms and the nuns'
house, its play yard often bustling into noisy excitement. Once upon a time Catherine and Alicia had
played there themselves, hardly noticing the house
across the road, blue then also.

'You're all right?' Alicia said on the evening of
the funeral, when together they cleared up the
glasses sherry had been drunk from, and cups and
saucers. On the sideboard in the dining room the
stoppers of the decanters had not yet been
replaced, crumbs not yet brushed from the din-
ing-table cloth.

'Yes, I'm all right,' Catherine said. In her girlhood
she had been pretty – slender and dark, and shyly
smiling, dimples in both cheeks. Alicia, taller, dark
also, had been considered the beauty of the town.
Now Catherine was greying, and plump about the
face, the joints of her fingers a little swollen. Alicia
was straight-backed, her beauty still recalled in
features that were classically proportioned, her hair
greyer than her sister's.

'Good of them all to come,' Catherine said.

'People liked Matthew.'

'Yes.'

For a moment Catherine felt the rising of her tears,
the first time since the morning of the death, but
stoically she held them in. Their marriage had not
gone. Their marriage was still there in children and in
grandchildren, in the voices that had spoken well of
it, in the bed they had shared, and in remembering.
The time being would not be endless; he had said
that, too. 'You're managing, Catherine?' people
asked, the same words often used, and she tried to

convey to them that strength still came from all there had been.

The day after the funeral Fagan from the solicitors' office explained to Catherine the contents of the few papers he brought to the house. It took ten minutes.

'I'll help you,' Alicia said later that same morning when Catherine mentioned Matthew's personal belongings. Clothes and shoes would be accepted gratefully by one of the charities with which Alicia was connected. The signet ring, the watch, the tie-pin, the matching fountain pen and propelling pencil were earmarked for the family, to be shared among Catherine's sons. Shaving things were thrown away.

Recalling the same sorting out of possessions at the time of her own loss, Alicia was in no way distressed. She had experienced little emotion when her husband's death occurred: for the last nineteen years of her marriage she had not loved him.

'You've been a strength,' Catherine said, for her sister had been that and more, looking after her as she used to, years ago, when they were children.

'Oh, no, no,' came Alicia's deprecation.

Thomas Pius John Leary was by trade a painter and decorator. He had, for this work, no special qualifications beyond experience; he brought to it no special skill. As a result, he was often accused of poor workmanship, which in turn led to disputes about payment. But he charged less than his competitors and so ensured a reasonably steady demand for his services. When for one reason or another the demand wasn't there he took on any kind of odd job he was offered.

Leary was middle-aged now, married, the father of six children. He was a small, wiry man with tight features, and bloodshot eyes, his spareness occasionally reminding people of a hedgerow animal they could not readily name. Sparse grey hair was brushed straight back from the narrow dome of his forehead. Two forefingers, thumbs, middle fingers, upper lip, and teeth were stained brown from cigarettes he manufactured with the aid of a small machine. Leary did not wear overalls when at work and was rarely encountered in clothes that did not bear splashes of paint.

It was in this condition, the damp end of a cigarette emerging from a cupped palm, that he presented himself to Catherine and Alicia one afternoon in November, six weeks after the death. He stood on the doorstep, declaring his regrets and sympathy in a low voice, not meeting Catherine's eye. In the time that had passed, other people had come to the door and said much the same thing; not many, only those who found it difficult to write a letter and considered the use of the telephone to be inappropriate in such circumstances. They'd made a brief statement and then had hurried off. Leary appeared inclined to linger.

'That's very good of you, Mr Leary,' Catherine said.

A few months earlier he had repainted the front of the house, the same pale blue. He had renewed the white gloss of the window frames. 'Poor Leary's desperate for work,' Matthew had said. 'Will we give the rogue a go?' Alicia had been against it, Leary not being a man she'd cared for when he'd done other jobs for them. Catherine, although she didn't much care for Leary either, felt sorry for anyone who was up against it.

'Could I step in for a minute?'

Across the street the convent children were running about in the play yard before their afternoon classes began. Still watching them, Catherine was aware of checking a frown that had begun to gather. He was looking for more work, she supposed, but there was no question of that. Alicia's misgivings had been justified; there'd been skimping on the amount and quality of the paint used, and inadequate preparation. 'We'll know not to do that again,' Matthew had said. Besides, there wasn't anything else that required attention at present.

'Of course,' Catherine stood aside while Leary passed into the long, narrow hall. She led the way down it, to the kitchen because it was warm there. Alicia was polishing the cutlery at the table, a task she undertook once a month.

'Sit down, Mr Leary,' Catherine invited, pulling a chair out for him.

'I was saying I was sorry,' he said to Alicia. 'If there's any way I can assist at all, any little job, I'm always there.'

'It's kind of you, Mr Leary,' Catherine said swiftly, in case her sister responded more tartly.

'I knew him since we were lads. He used to be at the Christian Brothers'.'

'Yes.'

'Great old days.'

He seemed embarrassed. He wanted to say something but was having difficulty. One hand went into a pocket of his jacket. Catherine watched it playing with the little contrivance he used for rolling his cigarettes. But the hand came out empty. Nervously, it was rubbed against its partner.

'It's awkward,' Leary said.

'What's awkward, Mr Leary?'

'It isn't easy, how to put it to you. I didn't come before because of your trouble.'

Alicia laid down the cloth with which she had been applying Goddard's Silver Polish to the cutlery, and Catherine watched her sister's slow, deliberate movements as she shined the last of the forks, and then drew off her pink rubber gloves and placed them one on top of the other, beside her. Alicia could sense something; she often had a way of knowing what was coming next.

'I don't know are you aware,' Leary enquired, addressing only Catherine, 'it wasn't paid for?'

'What wasn't?'

'The job I done for you.'

'You don't mean painting the front?'

'I do, ma'am.'

'But of course it was paid for.'

He sighed softly. An outstanding bill was an embarrassment, he said. Because of the death it was an embarrassment.

'My husband paid for the work that was done.'

'Ah no, no.'

The frown Catherine had checked a few moments ago wrinkled her forehead. She knew the bill had been paid. She knew because Matthew had said

Leary would want cash, and she had taken the money out of her own Irish Nationwide account, since she had easy access to it. 'I'll see you right at the end of the month,' Matthew had promised. It was an arrangement they often had; the building-society account in her name existed for this kind of thing.

'Two hundred and twenty-six pounds is the extent of the damage.' Leary smiled shiftily. 'With the discount for cash.'

She didn't tell him she'd withdrawn the money herself. That wasn't his business. She watched the extreme tip of his tongue licking his upper lip. He wiped his mouth with the back of a paint-stained hand. Softly, Alicia was replacing forks and spoons in the cutlery container.

'It was September the account was sent out. The wife does all that type of thing.'

'The bill was paid promptly. My husband always paid bills promptly.'

She remembered the occasion perfectly. 'I'll bring it down to him now,' Matthew had said, glancing across the kitchen at the clock. Every evening he walked down to McKenny's bar and remained there for three-quarters of an hour or so, depending on the company. That evening he'd have gone the long way round, by French Street, in order to call in at the Learys' house, in Brady's Lane. Before he left he had taken the notes from the brown Nationwide envelope and counted them slowly, just as she herself had done earlier. She'd seen the bill in his hand. 'Chancing his arm with the tax man,' she remembered his remarking lightly, a reference to Leary's preference for cash.

On his return he would have hung his cap on its
hook in the scullery passage and settled down at the
kitchen table with the *Evening Press*, which he bought
in Healy's sweetshop on his way back from McKenny's. He went to the public house for conversation as
much as anything, and afterwards passed on to Alicia
and herself any news he had gleaned. Bottled
Smithwick's was his drink.

'D'you remember it?' Catherine appealed to her
sister, because although she could herself so clearly
recall Matthew's departure from the house on that
particular September evening, his return eluded her.
It lay smothered somewhere beneath the evening
routine, nothing making it special, as the banknotes
in the envelope had made the other.

'I remember talk about money,' Alicia recalled,
'earlier that day. If I've got it right, I was out at the
Legion of Mary in the evening.'

'A while back the wife noticed the way the bill
was unpaid,' Leary went on, having paused politely
to hear these recollections.

'"It's the death that's in it," she said. She'd have
eaten the face off me if I'd bothered you in your
trouble.'

'Exuse me,' Catherine said.

She left the kitchen and went to look on the
spike in the side cupboard in the passage, where all
receipts were kept. This one should have been close
to the top, but it wasn't. It wasn't farther down
either. It wasn't in the cupboard drawers. She went
through the contents of three box files in case it
had been bundled into one in error. Again she
didn't find it.

She returned to the kitchen with the next best thing: the Nationwide Building Society account book. She opened it and placed it in front of Leary. She pointed at the entry that recorded the withdrawal of two hundred and twenty-six pounds. She could tell that there had been no conversation in her absence. Leary would have tried to get some kind of talk going, but Alicia wouldn't have responded.

'September the eighth,' Catherine said, emphasising the printed date with a forefinger. 'A Wednesday, it was.'

In silence Leary perused the entry. He shook his head. The tight features of his face tightened even more, bunching together into a knot of bewilderment. Catherine, glanced at her sister. He was putting it on, Alicia's expression indicated.

'The money was taken out, all right,' Leary said eventually. 'Did he put it to another use in that case?'

'Another use?'

'Did you locate a receipt, missus?'

He spoke softly, not in the cagey, underhand tone of someone attempting to get something for nothing. Catherine was still standing. He turned his head to one side in order to squint up at her. He sounded apologetic, but all that could be put on also.

'I brought the receipt book over with me,' he said.

He handed it to her, a fat, greasy notebook with a grey marbled cover that had 'The Challenge Receipt Book' printed on it. Blue carbon paper protruded from the dog-eared pages.

'Any receipt that's issued would have a copy left behind here,' he said, speaking now to Alicia, across the table. 'The top copy for the customer, the carbon for ourselves. You couldn't do business without you keep a record of receipts.'

He stood up then. He opened the book and displayed its unused pages, each with the same printed heading: 'In account with T. P. Leary.' He showed Catherine how the details of a bill were recorded on the flimsy page beneath the carbon sheet and how, when a bill was paid, acknowledgement was recorded also: 'Paid with thanks,' with the date and the careful scrawl of Mrs Leary's signature. He passed the receipt book to Alicia, pointing out these details to her also.

'Anything could have happened to that receipt,' Alicia said. 'In the circumstances.'

'If a receipt was issued, missus, there'd be a record of it here.'

Alicia placed the receipt book beside the much slimmer building-society book on the pale surface of the table. Leary's attention remained with the former, his scrutiny an emphasis of the facts it contained. The evidence offered otherwise was not for him to comment upon: so the steadiness of his gaze insisted.

'My husband counted those notes at this very table,' Catherine said. 'He took them out of the brown envelope that they were put into at the Nationwide.'

'It's a mystery so.'

It wasn't any such thing; there was no mystery whatsoever. The bill had been paid. Both sisters knew that; in their different ways they guessed that Leary – and presumably his wife as well – had planned this dishonesty as soon as they realised that death had given them the opportunity. Matthew had obliged them by paying cash so that they could defraud the taxation authorities. He had further obliged them by dying.

Catherine said, 'My husband walked out of this house with that envelope in his pocket. Are you telling me he didn't reach you?'

'Was he robbed? Would it be that? You hear terrible things these days.'

'Oh, for heaven's sake!'

Leary wagged his head in his meditative way. It was unlikely certainly, he agreed. Anyone robbed would have gone to the Guards. Anyone robbed would have mentioned it when he came back to the house again.

'The bill was paid, Mr Leary.'

'All the same, we have to go by the receipt. At the heel of the hunt there's the matter of a receipt.'

Alicia shook her head. Either a receipt wasn't issued in the first place, she said, or else it had been mislaid. 'There's a confusion when a person dies,' she said.

If Catherine had been able to produce the receipt Leary would have blamed his wife. He'd have blandly stated that she'd got her wires crossed. He'd have said the first thing that came into his head and then have gone away.

'The only thing is,' he said instead, 'a sum like that is sizeable. I couldn't afford to let it go.'

Both Catherine and Alicia had seen Mrs Leary in the shops, red-haired, like a tinker, a bigger woman than her husband, probably the brains of the two. The Learys were liars and worse than liars; the chance had come and the temptation had been too much for

them. 'Ah, sure, those two have plenty,' the woman
would have said. The sisters wondered if the Learys
had tricked the bereaved before, and imagined they
had.

Leary said, 'It's hard on a man that's done work for
you.'

Catherine moved towards the kitchen door. Leary
ambled after her down the hall. She remembered the
evening more clearly even than a while ago. A
Wednesday it definitely had been, the day of the
Sweetman girl's wedding; and also, it came back to
her, Alicia hurrying out on her Legion of Mary
business. There'd been talk in McKenny's about
the wedding, the unusual choice of mid-week,
which apparently had something to do with visitors
coming from America. She opened the hall door in
silence. Across the street, beyond the silver-coloured
railings, the children were still running about in the
convent yard. Watery sunlight lightened the un-
adorned concrete of the classrooms and the nuns'
house.

'What'll I do?' Leary asked, wide-eyed, bloodshot,
squinting at her.

Catherine said nothing.

They talked about it. It could be, Alicia said, that the
receipt had remained in one of Matthew's pockets,
that a jacket she had disposed of to one of her
charities had later found itself in the Learys' hands,
having passed through a jumble sale. She could
imagine Mrs Leary coming across it, and the temptation being too much. Leary was as weak as water, she
said, adding that the tinker wife was a woman who

never looked you in the eye. Foxy-faced and furtive, Mrs Leary pushed a ramshackle pram about the streets, her ragged children cowering in her presence. It was she who would have removed the flimsy carbon copy from the soiled receipt book. Leary would have been putty in her hands.

In the kitchen they sat down at the table, from which Alicia had cleared away the polished cutlery. Matthew had died as tidily as he'd lived, Alicia said: all his life he'd been meticulous. The Learys had failed to remember that. If it came to a court of law the Learys wouldn't have a leg to stand on, with the written evidence that the precise amount taken out of the building society matched the amount of the bill, and further evidence in Matthew's reputation for promptness about settling debts.

'What I'm wondering is,' Alicia said, 'should we go to the Guards?'

'The Guards?'

'He shouldn't have come here like that.'

That evening there arrived a bill for the amount quoted by Leary marked 'Account rendered'. It was dropped through the letter box and was discovered the next morning beneath the *Irish Independent* on the hall doormat.

'The little twister!' Alicia furiously exclaimed.

From the road outside the house came the morning commands of the convent girl in charge of the crossing to the school: 'Get ready!' 'Prepare to cross!' 'Cross now!' Impertinence had been added to dishonesty, Alicia declared in outraged tones. It was as though it had never been pointed out to Leary that Matthew had left the house on the evening in

question with two hundred and twenty-six pounds in
an envelope, that Leary's attention had never been
drawn to the clear evidence of the building-society
entry.

'It beats me,' Catherine said, and in the hall Alicia
turned sharply and said it was as clear as day. Again
she mentioned going to the Guards. A single visit
from Sergeant McBride, she maintained, and the
Learys would abandon their cheek. From the play
yard the yells of the girls increased as more girls
arrived there, and then the handbell sounded; a
moment later there was silence.

'I'm only wondering,' Catherine said, 'if there's
some kind of mistake.'

'There's no mistake, Catherine.'

Alicia didn't comment further. She led the way to
the kitchen and half-filled a saucepan with water for
their two boiled eggs. Catherine cut bread for toast.
When she and Alicia had been girls in that same play
yard she hadn't known of Matthew's existence. Years
passed before she even noticed him, at Mass one
Saturday night. And it was ages before he first invited
her to go out with him, for a walk the first time, and
then for a drive.

'What d'you think happened, then?' Alicia asked.
'That Matthew bet the money on a dog? That he
owed it for drink consumed? Have sense, Catherine.'

Had it been Alicia's own husband whom Leary
had charged with negligence, there would have been
no necessary suspension of disbelief: feckless and a
nuisance, involved during his marriage with at least
one other woman in the town, frequenter of
racecourses and dog tracks and bars, he had ended

in an early grave. This shared thought – that
behaviour which was ludicrous when attached to
Matthew had been as natural in Alicia's husband as
breathing – was there between the sisters, but was not
mentioned.

'If Father Cahill got Leary on his own,' Alicia
began, but Catherine interrupted. She didn't want
that, she said; she didn't want other people brought
into this, not even Father Cahill. She didn't want a
fuss about whether or not her husband had paid a
bill.

'You'll get more of these,' Alicia warned, laying a
finger on the envelope that had been put through the
letter box. 'They'll keep coming.'

'Yes.'

In the night Catherine had lain awake, wondering
if Matthew had maybe lost the money on his walk to
the Learys' house that evening, if he'd put his hand in
his pocket and found it wasn't there and then been
too ashamed to say. It wasn't like him; it didn't make
much more sense than thinking he had been a
secretive man, with private shortcomings all the
years she'd been married to him. When Alicia's
husband died Matthew had said it was hard to feel
sorry, and she'd agreed. Three times Alicia had been
left on her own, for periods that varied in length, and
on each occasion they'd thought the man was gone
for good; but he returned and Alicia always took him
back. Of course Matthew hadn't lost the money: it
was as silly to think that as to wonder if he'd been a
gambler.

'In case they'd try it on anyone else,' Alicia was
saying, 'isn't it better they should be shown up? Is a

man who'd get up to that kind of game safe to be left in people's houses the way a workman is?'

That morning they didn't mention the matter again. They washed up the breakfast dishes and then Catherine went out to the shops, which was always her chore, while Alicia cleaned the stairs and the hall, the day being a Thursday. As Catherine made her way through the familiar streets, and while Mr Deegan sliced bacon for her and then while Gilligan greeted her in the hardware, she thought about the journey her husband had made that Wednesday evening in September. Involuntarily, she glanced into Healy's, where he had bought the *Evening Press*, and into McKenny's bar. Every evening except Sunday, he had brought back the news, bits of gossip, anything he'd heard. It was at this time, too, that he went to confession, on such occasions leaving the house half an hour earlier.

In French Street, a countrywoman opened her car door without looking and knocked a cyclist over. 'Ah, no harm done,' the youth on the bicycle said. He was the delivery boy for Lawless, the West Street butcher, the last delivery boy in the town. 'Sure, I never saw him at all,' the countrywoman protested to Catherine as she went by. The car door was dinged, but the woman said what did it matter if the lad was all right?

Culliney, the traveller from Limerick Shirts, was in town that day. Matthew had always bought his shirts direct from Culliney, the same striped pattern, the stripe blue or brown. Culliney had his measurements, the way he had the measurements of men all over Munster and Connacht, which was his area.

Catherine could tell when she saw Culliney coming towards her that he didn't know about the death, and she braced herself to tell him. When she did so he put a hand on her arm and spoke in a whisper, saying that Matthew had been a good man. If there was anything he could ever do, he said, if there was any way he could help. More people said that than didn't.

It was then that Catherine saw Mrs Leary. The housepainter's wife was pushing her pram, a child holding on to it as she advanced. Catherine crossed to the other side of the street, wondering if the woman had seen her and suspecting she had. In Jerety's she selected a pan loaf from the yesterday's, since neither she nor Alicia liked fresh bread and yesterday's was always reduced. When she emerged, Mrs Leary was not to be seen.

'Nothing, only a woman knocked young Nallen off his bike,' she reported to Alicia when she returned to the house. 'Is he a Nallen, that boy of Lawless's?'

'Or a Keane, is he? Big head on him?'

'I don't think he's a Keane. Someone told me a Nallen. Whoever he is, there's no harm done.' She didn't say she'd seen Mrs Leary, because she didn't want to raise again the subject of what had occurred. She knew that Alicia was right: the bill would keep coming unless she did something about it. Once they'd set out on the course they'd chosen, why should the Learys give up? Alicia didn't refer to the Learys either, but that evening, when they had switched off the television and were preparing to go to bed, Catherine said, 'I think I'll pay them. Simplest, that would be.'

With her right hand on the newel of the banister, about to ascend the stairs, Alicia stared in disbelief at her sister. When Catherine nodded and continued on her way to the kitchen she followed her.

'But you can't.' Alicia stood in the doorway while Catherine washed and rinsed the cups they'd drunk their bedtime tea from. 'You can't just pay them what isn't owing.'

Catherine turned the tap off at the sink and set the cups to drain, slipping the accompanying saucers between the plastic bars of the drainer. Tomorrow she would withdraw the same sum from the building-society account and take it herself to the Learys in Brady's Lane. She would stand there while a receipt was issued.

'Catherine, you can't hand out more than two hundred pounds.'

'I'd rather.'

As she spoke, she changed her mind about the detail of the payment. Matthew had been obliging Leary by paying cash, but there was no need to oblige him anymore. She would arrange for the Irish Nationwide to draw a cheque payable to T. P. Leary. She would bring it round to the Learys instead of a wad of notes.

'They've taken you for a fool,' Alicia said.

'I know they have.'

'Leary should go behind bars. You're aiding and abetting him. Have sense, woman.'

A disappointment rose in Alicia, bewildering and muddled. The death of her own husband had brought an end, and her expectation had been that widowhood for her sister would be the same. Her expectation had been that in their shared state they would be as once they were, now that marriage was over, packed away with their similar mourning clothes. Yet almost palpable in the kitchen was Catherine's resolve that what still remained for her should not be damaged by a fuss of protest over a confidence trick. The Guards investigating clothes sold at a jumble sale, strangers asked if a house-painter's wife had bought this garment or that, private intimacies made public: Catherine was paying money in case, somehow, the memory of her husband should be accidentally tarnished. And knowing her sister well, Alicia knew that this resolve would become more stubborn as time passed. It would mark and influence her sister; it would breed new eccentricities in her. If Leary had not come that day there would have been something else.

'You'd have the man back, I suppose?' Alicia said, trying to hurt and knowing she succeeded. 'You'd have him back in to paint again, to lift the bits and pieces from your dressing table?'

'It's not to do with Leary.'

'What's it to do with then?'

'Let's leave it.'

Hanging up a tea towel, Catherine noticed that her fingers were trembling. They never quarrelled; even in childhood they hadn't. In all the years Alicia had lived in the house she had never spoken in this unpleasant way, her voice rudely raised.

'They're walking all over you, Catherine.'

'Yes.'

They did not speak again, not even to say good-night. Alicia closed her bedroom door, telling herself

crossly that her expectation had not been a greedy
one. She had been unhappy in her foolish marriage,
and after it she had been beholden in this house.
Although it ran against her nature to do so, she had
borne her lot without complaint; why should she not
fairly have hoped that in widowhood they would
again be sisters first of all?

In her bedroom Catherine undressed and for a
moment caught a glimpse of the nakedness in her
dressing-table looking glass. She missed her husband's warmth in bed, a hand holding hers before
they slept, that last embrace, and sometimes in the
night his voice saying he loved her. She pulled her
nightdress on, then knelt to pray before she turned
the light out.

Some instinct, vague and imprecise, drew her in
the darkness on to the territory of Alicia's disappointment. In the family photographs – some
clearly defined, some now drained of detail,
affected by the sun – they were the sisters they
had been: Alicia beautiful, confidently smiling;
Catherine in her care. Catherine's first memory
was of a yellow flower, and sunlight, and a white
cloth hat put on her head. That flower was a
cowslip, Alicia told her afterwards, and said that
they'd gone with their mother to the ruins by the
river that day, that it was she who found the
cowslip. 'Look, Catherine,' she'd said. 'A lovely
flower.' Catherine had watched in admiration
when Alicia paraded in her First Communion
dress, and later when boys paid her attention.
Alicia was the important one, responsible, reli-

able, right about things, offered the deference
that was an older sister's due. She'd been a
strength, Catherine said after Matthew's funeral,
and Alicia was pleased, even though she shook her
head.

Catherine dropped into sleep after half an hour
of wakefulness. She woke up a few times in the
night, on each occasion to find her thoughts full of
the decision she had made, and of her sister's
outraged face, the two tiny patches of red that
had come into it, high up on her cheeks, the snap
of disdain in her eyes. 'A laughing-stock,' Alicia
said in a dream. 'No more than a laughing-stock,
Catherine.'

As Catherine lay there she imagined the silent
breakfast there would be, and saw herself walking to
Brady's Lane, and Leary fiddling with his cigarette-
making gadget, and Mrs Leary in fluffy pink
slippers, her stockingless legs mottled from being
too close to the fire. Tea would be offered, but
Catherine would refuse it. 'A decenter man never
stood in a pair of shoes,' Leary could be counted
upon to state.

She did not sleep again. She watched the darkness
lighten, heard the first cars of the day pass on the road
outside the house. By chance, a petty dishonesty had
given death its due, which Alicia had cheated it of
when she was widowed herself. It took from her
now, as it had not then.

Catherine knew this intuition was no trick of
her tired mind. While they were widows in her
house Alicia's jealousy would be the truth they
shared, with tonight's few moments of its presence

lingering insistently. Widows were widows first. Catherine would mourn, and feel in solitude the warmth of love. For Alicia there was the memory of her beauty.

Death in Jerusalem

'Till then,' Father Paul said, leaning out of the train window. 'Till Jerusalem, Francis.'

'Please God, Paul.' As he spoke the Dublin train began to move and his brother waved from the window and he waved back, a modest figure on the platform. Everyone said Francis might have been a priest as well, meaning that Francis's quietness and meditative disposition had an air of the cloister about them. But Francis contented himself with the running of Conary's hardware business, which his mother had run until she was too old for it. 'Are we game for the Holy Land next year?' Father Paul had asked that July. 'Will we go together, Francis?' He had brushed aside all Francis's protestations, all attempts to explain that the shop could not be left, that their mother would be confused by the absence of Francis from the house. Rumbustiously he'd pointed out that there was their sister Kitty, who was in charge of the household of which Francis and their mother were part and whose husband, Myles, could surely be trusted to look after the shop for a single fortnight. For thirty years, ever since he was seven, Francis had wanted to go to the Holy Land. He had savings which he'd never spent a penny of: you couldn't take them with you, Father Paul had more than once stated that July.

On the platform Francis watched until the train could no longer be seen, his thoughts still with his brother. The priest's ruddy countenance smiled again behind cigarette smoke; his bulk remained impressive in his clerical clothes, the collar pinching the flesh of his neck, his black shoes scrupulously polished. There were freckles on the backs of his large, strong hands; he had a fine head of hair, grey and crinkly. In an hour and a half's time the train would creep into Dublin, and he'd take a taxi. He'd spend a night in the Gresham Hotel, probably falling in with another priest, having a drink or two, maybe playing a game of bridge after his meal. That was his brother's way and always had been – an extravagant, easy kind of way, full of smiles and good humour. It was what had taken him to America and made him successful there. In order to raise money for the church that he and Father Steigmuller intended to build before 1980 he took parties of the well-to-do from San Francisco to Rome and Florence, to Chartres and Seville and the Holy Land. He was good at raising money, not just for the church but for the boys' home of which he was president, and for the Hospital of Our Saviour, and for St Mary's Old People's Home on the west side of the city. But every July he flew back to Ireland, to the town in Co. Tipperary where his mother and brother and sister still lived. He stayed in the house above the shop which he might have inherited himself on the death of his father, which he'd rejected in favour of the religious life. Mrs Conary was eighty now. In the shop she sat silently behind the counter, in a corner by the chicken-wire, wearing only clothes that were black. In the evenings she sat with Francis in the lace-curtained sitting-room, while the rest of the family occupied the kitchen. It was for her sake most of all that Father Paul made the journey every summer, considering it his duty.

Walking back to the town from the station, Francis was aware that he was missing his brother. Father Paul was fourteen years older and in childhood had often taken the place of their father, who had died when Francis was five. His brother had possessed an envied strength and knowledge; he'd been a hero, quite often worshipped, an example of success. In later life he had become an example of generosity as well: ten years ago he'd taken their mother to Rome, and their sister Kitty and her husband two years later; he'd paid the expenses when their sister Edna had gone to Canada; he'd assisted two nephews to make a start in America. In childhood Francis hadn't possessed his brother's healthy freckled face, just as in middle age he didn't have his ruddy complexion and his stoutness and his easiness with people. Francis was slight, his sandy hair receding, his face rather pale. His breathing was sometimes laboured because of wheeziness in the chest. In the ironmonger's shop he wore a brown cotton coat.

'Hullo, Mr Conary,' a woman said to him in the main street of the town. 'Father Paul's gone off, has he?'

'Yes, he's gone again.'

'I'll pray for his journey so,' the woman promised, and Francis thanked her.

A year went by. In San Francisco another wing of the boys' home was completed, another target was reached in Father Paul and Father Steigmuller's fund for the church they planned to have built by 1980. In the town in Co. Tipperary there were baptisms and burial services and First Communions. Old Loughlin, a farmer from Bansha, died in McSharry's grocery and bar, having gone there to celebrate a good price he'd got for a heifer. Clancy, from behind the counter in Doran's drapery, married Maureen Talbot; Mr Nolan's plasterer married Miss Carron; Johneen Meagher married Seamus in the chip-shop, under pressure from her family to do so. A local horse, from the stables on the Limerick road, was said to be an entry for the Fairyhouse Grand National, but it turned out not to be true. Every evening of that year Francis sat with his mother in the lace-curtained sitting-room above the shop. Every weekday she sat in her corner by the chicken-wire, watching while he counted out screws and weighed staples, or advised about yard brushes or tap-washers. Occasionally, on a Saturday, he visited the three Christian Brothers who lodged with Mrs Shea and afterwards he'd tell his mother about how the authority was slipping these days from the nuns and the Christian Brothers, and how Mrs Shea's elderly maid, Ita, couldn't see to cook the food any more. His mother would nod and hardly ever speak. When he told a joke – what young Hogan had said when he'd found a nail in his egg or how Ita had put mint sauce into a jug with milk in it – she never laughed, and looked at him in surprise when he laughed himself. But Dr Foran said it was best to keep her cheered up.

All during that year Francis talked to her about his forthcoming visit to the Holy Land, endeavouring to make her understand that for a fortnight next spring he would be away from the house and the shop. He'd been away before for odd days, but that was when she'd been younger. He used to visit an aunt in Tralee, but three years ago the aunt had died and he hadn't left the town since.

Francis and his mother had always been close. Before his birth two daughters had died in infancy, and his very survival had often struck Mrs Conary as a gift. He had always been her favourite, the one among her children whom she often considered least able to stand on his own two feet. It was just like Paul to have gone blustering off to San Francisco instead of remaining in Co. Tipperary. It was just like Kitty to have married a useless man. 'There's not a girl in the town who'd touch him,' she'd said to her daughter at the time, but Kitty had been headstrong and adamant, and there was Myles now, doing nothing whatsoever except cleaning other people's windows for a pittance and placing bets in Donovan's the turf accountant's. It was the shop and the arrangement Kitty had with Francis and her mother that kept her and the children going, three of whom had already left the town, which in Mrs Conary's opinion they mightn't have done if they'd had a better type of father. Mrs Conary often wondered what her own two babies who'd died might have grown up into, and imagined they might have been like Francis, about whom she'd never had a moment's worry. Not in a million years would he give you the feeling that he was too big for his boots, like Paul sometimes did with his lavishness and his big talk of America. He wasn't silly like Kitty, or so sinful you couldn't forgive him, the way you couldn't forgive Edna, even though she was dead and buried in Toronto.

Francis understood how his mother felt about the family. She'd had a hard life, left a widow early on, trying to do the best she could for everyone. In turn he did his best to compensate for the struggles and disappointments she'd suffered, cheering her in the evenings while Kitty and Myles and the youngest of their children watched the television in the kitchen. His mother had ignored the existence of Myles for ten years, ever since the day he'd taken money out of the till to pick up the odds on Gusty Spirit at Phoenix Park. And although Francis got on well enough with Myles he quite understood that there should be a long aftermath to that day. There'd been a terrible row in the kitchen, Kitty screaming at Myles and Myles telling lies and Francis trying to keep them calm, saying they'd give the old woman a heart attack.

She didn't like upsets of any kind, so all during the year before he was to visit the Holy Land Francis read the New Testament to her in order to prepare her. He talked to her about Bethlehem and Nazareth and the miracle of the loaves and fishes and all the other miracles. She kept nodding, but he often wondered if she didn't assume he was just casually referring to episodes in the Bible. As a child he had listened to such talk himself, with awe and fascination, imagining the walking on the water and the temptation in the wilderness. He had imagined the cross carried to Calvary and the rock rolled back from the tomb, and the rising from the dead on the third day. That he was now to walk in such places seemed extraordinary to him, and he wished his mother was younger so that she could appreciate his good fortune and share it with him when she received the postcards he intended, every day, to send her. But her eyes seemed always to tell him that he was making a mistake, that somehow he was making a fool of himself by doing such a showy thing as going to the Holy Land. *I have the entire itinerary mapped out*, his brother wrote from San Francisco. *There's nothing we'll miss.*

It was the first time Francis had been in an aeroplane. He flew by Aer Lingus from Dublin to London and then changed to an El Al flight to Tel Aviv. He was nervous and he found it exhausting. All the time he seemed to be eating, and it was strange being among so many people he didn't know. 'You will taste honey such as never before,' an Israeli businessman in the seat next to his assured him. 'And Galilean figs. Make certain to taste Galilean figs.' Make certain too, the businessman went on, to experience Jerusalem by night and in the early dawn. He urged Francis to see places he had never heard of, Yad Va-Shem, the treasures of the Shrine of the Book. He urged him to honour the martyrs of Masada and to learn a few words of Hebrew as a token of respect. He told him of a shop where he could buy mementoes and warned him against Arab street traders.

'The hard man, how are you?' Father Paul said at
Tel Aviv airport, having flown in from San Francisco
the day before. Father Paul had had a drink or two
and he suggested another when they arrived at the
Plaza Hotel in Jerusalem. It was half past nine in the
evening. 'A quick little nightcap,' Father Paul
insisted, 'and then hop into bed with you, Francis.'
They sat in an enormous open lounge with low,
round tables and square modern armchairs. Father
Paul said it was the bar.

They had said what had to be said in the car from
Tel Aviv to Jerusalem. Father Paul had asked about
their mother, and Kitty and Myles. He'd asked about
other people in the town, old Canon Mahon and
Sergeant Murray. He and Father Steigmuller had had
a great year of it, he reported: as well as everything
else, the boys' home had turned out two tip-top
footballers. 'We'll start on a tour at half-nine in the
morning,' he said. 'I'll be sitting having breakfast at
eight.'

Francis went to bed and Father Paul ordered
another whisky, with ice. To his great disappointment there was no Irish whiskey in the
hotel so he'd had to content himself with Haig.
He fell into conversation with an American
couple, making them promise that if they were
ever in Ireland they wouldn't miss out Co.
Tipperary. At eleven o'clock the barman said
he was wanted at the reception desk and when
Father Paul went there and announced himself he
was given a message in an envelope. It was a
telegram that had come, the girl said in poor
English. Then she shook her head, saying it was a

telex. He opened the envelope and learn that
Mrs Conary had died.

Francis fell asleep immediately and dreamed that he
was a boy again, out fishing with a friend whom he
couldn't how identify.

On the telephone Father Paul ordered whisky and
ice to be brought to his room. Before drinking it he
took his jacket off and knelt by his bed to pray for his
mother's salvation. When he'd completed the prayers
he walked slowly up and down the length of the
room, occasionally sipping at his whisky. He argued
with himself and finally arrived at a decision.

For breakfast they had scrambled eggs that looked
like yellow ice-cream, and orange juice that was
delicious. Francis wondered about bacon, but Father
Paul explained that bacon was not readily available in
Israel.

'Did you sleep all right?' Father Paul inquired.
'Did you have the jet-lag?'

'Jet-lag?'

'A tiredness you get after jet flights. It'd knock you
out for days.'

'Ah, I slept great, Paul.'

'Good man.'

They lingered over breakfast. Father Paul reported
a little more of what had happened in his parish
during the year, in particular about the two young
footballers from the boys' home. Francis told about
the decline in the cooking at Mrs Shea's boarding-
house, as related to him by the three Christian
Brothers. 'I have a car laid on,' Father Paul said,

and twenty minutes later they walked out into the
Jerusalem sunshine.

The hired car stopped on the way to the walls of
the Old City. It drew into a lay-by at Father Paul's
request and the two men got out and looked across a
wide valley dotted with houses and olive trees. A
road curled along the distant slope opposite. 'The
Mount of Olives,' Father Paul said. 'And that's the
road to Jericho.' He pointed more particularly. 'You
see that group of eight big olives? Just off the road,
where the church is?'

Francis thought he did, but was not sure. There
were so many olive trees, and more than one church.
He glanced at his brother's pointing finger and
followed its direction with his glance.

'The Garden of Gethsemane,' Father Paul said.

Francis did not say anything. He continued to gaze
at the distant church, with the clump of olive trees
beside it. Wild flowers were profuse on the slopes of
the valley, smears of orange and blue on land that
looked poor. Two Arab women herded goats.

'Could we see it closer?' he asked, and his brother
said that definitely they would. They returned to the
waiting car and Father Paul ordered it to the Gate of
St Stephen.

Tourists heavy with cameras thronged the Via
Dolorosa. Brown, barefoot children asked for alms.
Stall-keepers pressed their different wares: cotton
dresses, metal-ware, mementoes, sacred goods. 'Get
out of the way,' Father Paul kept saying to them,
genially laughing to show he wasn't being abrupt.
Francis wanted to stand still and close his eyes, to
visualize for a moment the carrying of the Cross. But

the ceremony of the Stations, familiar to him for as long as he could remember, was unreal. Try as he would, Christ's journey refused to enter his imagination, and his own plain church seemed closer to the heart of the matter than the noisy lane he was now being jostled on. 'God damn it, of course it's genuine,' an angry American voice proclaimed, in reply to a shriller voice which insisted that cheating had taken place. The voices argued about a piece of wood, neat beneath plastic in a little box, a sample or not of the Cross that had been carried.

They arrived at the Church of the Holy Sepulchre, and at the Chapel of the Nailing to the Cross, where they prayed. They passed through the Chapel of the Angel, to the tomb of Christ. Nobody spoke in the marble cell, but when they left the church Francis overheard a quiet man with spectacles saying it was unlikely that a body would have been buried within the walls of the city. They walked to Hezekiah's Pool and out of the Old City at the Jaffa Gate, where their hired car was waiting for them. 'Are you peckish?' Father Paul asked, and although Francis said he wasn't they returned to the hotel.

Delay funeral till Monday was the telegram Father Paul had sent. There was an early flight on Sunday, in time for an afternoon one from London to Dublin. With luck there'd be a late train on Sunday evening and if there wasn't they'd have to fix a car. Today was Tuesday. It would give them four and a half days. *Funeral eleven Monday* the telegram at the reception desk now confirmed. 'Ah, isn't that great?' he said to himself, bundling the telegram up.

'Will we have a small one?' he suggested in the open area that was the bar. 'Or better still a big one.' He laughed. He was in good spirits in spite of the death that had taken place. He gestured at the barman, wagging his head and smiling jovially.

His face had reddened in the morning sun; there were specks of sweat on his forehead and his nose. 'Bethlehem this afternoon,' he laid down. 'Unless the jet-lag . . .?'

'I haven't got the jet-lag.'

In the Nativity Boutique Francis bought for his mother a small metal plate with a fish on it. He had stood for a moment, scarcely able to believe it, on the spot where the manger had been, in the Church of the Nativity. As in the Via Dolorosa it had been difficult to clear his mind of the surroundings that now were present: the exotic Greek Orthodox trappings, the foreign-looking priests, the oriental smell. Gold, frankincense and myrrh, he'd kept thinking, for somehow the church seemed more the church of the kings than of Joseph and Mary and their child. Afterwards they returned to Jerusalem, to the Tomb of the Virgin and the Garden of Gethsemane. 'It could have been anywhere,' he heard the quiet, bespectacled sceptic remarking in Gethsemane. 'They're only guessing.'

Father Paul rested in the late afternoon, lying down on his bed with his jacket off. He slept from half past five until a quarter past seven and awoke refreshed. He picked up the telephone and asked for whisky and ice to be brought up and when it arrived he undressed and had a bath, relaxing in the warm water

with the drink on a ledge in the tiled wall beside him.
There would be time to take in Nazareth and Galilee.
He was particularly keen that his brother should see
Galilee because Galilee had atmosphere and was
beautiful. There wasn't, in his own opinion, very
much to Nazareth but it would be a pity to miss it all
the same. It was at the Sea of Galilee that he intended
to tell his brother of their mother's death.

We've had a great day, Francis wrote on a postcard that
showed an aerial view of Jerusalem. *The Church of the
Holy Sepulchre, where Our Lord's tomb is, and Gethsemane
and Bethlehem. Paul's in great form.* He addressed it to his
mother, and then wrote other cards, to Kitty and Myles
and to the three Christian Brothers in Mrs Shea's, and
to Canon Mahon. He gave thanks that he was
privileged to be in Jerusalem. He read St Mark and
some of St Matthew. He said his rosary.

'Will we chance the wine?' Father Paul said at
dinner, not that wine was something he went in for,
but a waiter had come up and put a large padded
wine-list into his hand.

'Ah, no, no,' Francis protested, but already Father
Paul was running his eye down the listed bottles.

'Have you local wine?' he inquired of the waiter.
'A nice red one?'

The waiter nodded and hurried away, and Francis
hoped he wouldn't get drunk, the red wine on top of
the whisky he'd had in the bar before the meal. He'd
only had the one whisky, not being much used to it,
making it last through his brother's three.

'I heard some gurriers in the bar,' Father Paul said,
'making a great song and dance about the local red
wine.'

Wine made Francis think of the Holy Communion, but he didn't say so. He said the soup was delicious and he drew his brother's attention to the custom there was in the hotel of a porter ringing a bell and walking about with a person's name chalked on a little blackboard on the end of a rod.

'It's a way of paging you,' Father Paul explained. 'Isn't it nicer than bellowing out some fellow's name?' He smiled his easy smile, his eye beginning to water as a result of the few drinks he'd had. He was beginning to feel the strain: he kept thinking of their mother lying there, of what she'd say if she knew what he'd done, how she'd savagely upbraid him for keeping the fact from Francis. Out of duty and humanity he had returned each year to see her because, after all, you only had the one mother. But he had never cared for her.

Francis went for a walk after dinner. There were young soldiers with what seemed to be toy guns on the streets, but he knew the guns were real. In the shop windows there were television sets for sale, and furniture and clothes, just like anywhere else. There were advertisements for some film or other, two writhing women without a stitch on them, the kind of thing you wouldn't see in Co. Tipperary. 'You want something, sir?' a girl said, smiling at him with broken front teeth. The siren of a police car or an ambulance shrilled urgently near by. He shook his head at the girl. 'No, I don't want anything,' he said, and then realized what she had meant. She was small and very dark, no more than a child. He hurried on, praying for her.

When he returned to the hotel he found his
brother in the lounge with other people, two men
and two women. Father Paul was ordering a round
of drinks and called out to the barman to bring
another whisky. 'Ah, no, no,' Francis protested,
anxious to go to his room and to think about the
day, to read the New Testament and perhaps to write
a few more postcards. Music was playing, coming
from speakers that could not be seen.

'My brother Francis,' Father Paul said to the
people he was with, and the people all gave their
names, adding that they came from New York. 'I was
telling them about Tipp,' Father Paul said to his
brother, offering his packet of cigarettes around.

'You like Jerusalem, Francis?' one of the American
women asked him, and he replied that he hadn't
been able to take it in yet. Then, feeling that didn't
sound enthusiastic enough, he added that being there
was the experience of a lifetime.

Father Paul went on talking about Co. Tipperary and then spoke of his parish in San Francisco,
the boys' home and the two promising footballers,
the plans for the new church. The Americans
listened and in a moment the conversation drifted
on to the subject of their travels in England, their
visit to Istanbul and Athens, an argument they'd
had with the Customs at Tel Aviv. 'Well, I think
I'll hit the hay,' one of the men announced
eventually, standing up.

The others stood up too and so did Francis. Father
Paul remained where he was, gesturing again in the
direction of the barman. 'Sit down for a nightcap,' he
urged his brother.

'Ah, no, no –' Francis began.

'Bring us two more of those,' the priest ordered with a sudden abruptness, and the barman hurried away. 'Listen,' said Father Paul. 'I've something to tell you.'

After dinner, while Francis had been out on his walk, before he'd dropped into conversation with the Americans, Father Paul had said to himself that he couldn't stand the strain. It was the old woman stretched out above the hardware shop, as stiff as a board already, with the little lights burning in her room: he kept seeing all that, as if she wanted him to, as if she was trying to haunt him. Nice as the idea was, he didn't think he could continue with what he'd planned, with waiting until they got up to Galilee.

Francis didn't want to drink any more. He hadn't wanted the whisky his brother had ordered him earlier, nor the one the Americans had ordered for him. He didn't want the one that the barman now brought. He thought he'd just leave it there, hoping his brother wouldn't see it. He lifted the glass to his lips, but he managed not to drink any.

'A bad thing has happened,' Father Paul said.

'Bad? How d'you mean, Paul?'

'Are you ready for it?' He paused. Then he said, 'She died.'

Francis didn't know what he was talking about. He didn't know who was meant to be dead, or why his brother was behaving in an odd manner. He didn't like to think it but he had to: his brother wasn't fully sober.

'Our mother died,' Father Paul said. 'I'm after getting a telegram.'

The huge area that was the lounge of the Plaza Hotel, the endless tables and people sitting at them, the swiftly moving waiters and barmen seemed suddenly a dream. Francis had a feeling that he was not where he appeared to be, that he wasn't sitting with his brother, who was wiping his lips with a handkerchief. For a moment he appeared in his confusion to be struggling his way up the Via Dolorosa again, and then in the Nativity Boutique.

'Take it easy, boy,' his brother was saying. 'Take a mouthful of whisky.'

Francis didn't obey that injunction. He asked his brother to repeat what he had said, and Father Paul repeated that their mother had died.

Francis closed his eyes and tried as well to shut away the sounds around them. He prayed for the salvation of his mother's soul. 'Blessed Virgin, intercede,' his own voice said in his mind. 'Dear Mary, let her few small sins be forgiven.'

Having rid himself of his secret, Father Paul felt instant relief. With the best of intentions, it had been a foolish idea to think he could maintain the secret until they arrived in a place that was perhaps the most suitable in the world to hear about the death of a person who'd been close to you. He took a gulp of his whisky and wiped his mouth with his handkerchief again. He watched his brother, waiting for his eyes to open.

'When did it happen?' Francis asked eventually.

'Yesterday.'

'And the telegram only came – '

'It came last night, Francis. I wanted to save you the pain.'

'Save me? How could you save me? I sent her a postcard, Paul.'

'Listen to me, Francis – '

'How could you save me the pain?'

'I wanted to tell you when we got up to Galilee.'

Again Francis felt he was caught in the middle of a dream. He couldn't understand his brother: he couldn't understand what he meant by saying a telegram had come last night, why at a moment like this he was talking about Galilee. He didn't know why he was sitting in this noisy place when he should be back in Ireland.

'I fixed the funeral for Monday,' Father Paul said.

Francis nodded, not grasping the significance of this arrangement. 'We'll be back there this time tomorrow,' he said.

'No need for that, Francis. Sunday morning's time enough.'

'But she's dead – '

'We'll be there in time for the funeral.'

'We can't stay here if she's dead.'

It was this, Father Paul realized, he'd been afraid of when he'd argued with himself and made his plan. If he had knocked on Francis's door the night before, Francis would have wanted to return immediately without seeing a single stone of the land he had come so far to be moved by.

'We could go straight up to Galilee in the morning,' Father Paul said quietly. 'You'll find comfort in Galilee, Francis.'

But Francis shook his head. 'I want to be with her,' he said.

Father Paul lit another cigarette. He nodded at a hovering waiter, indicating his need of another drink.

He said to himself that he must keep his cool, an expression he was fond of.

'Take it easy, Francis,' he said.

'Is there a plane out in the morning? Can we make arrangements now?' He looked about him as if for a member of the hotel staff who might be helpful.

'No good'll be done by tearing off home, Francis. What's wrong with Sunday?'

'I want to be with her.'

Anger swelled within Father Paul. If he began to argue his words would become slurred: he knew that from experience. He must keep his cool and speak slowly and clearly, making a few simple points. It was typical of her, he thought, to die inconveniently.

'You've come all this way,' he said as slowly as he could without sounding peculiar. 'Why cut it any shorter than we need? We'll be losing a week anyway. She wouldn't want us to go back.'

'I think she would.'

He was right in that. Her possessiveness in her lifetime would have reached out across a dozen continents for Francis. She'd known what she was doing by dying when she had.

'I shouldn't have come,' Francis said. 'She didn't want me to come.'

'You're thirty-seven years of age, Francis.'

'I did wrong to come.'

'You did no such thing.'

The time he'd taken her to Rome she'd been difficult for the whole week, complaining about the food, saying everywhere was dirty. Whenever he'd spent anything she'd disapproved. All his life, Father Paul felt, he'd done his best for her. He had told her before anyone else when he'd decided to enter the priesthood, certain that she'd be pleased. 'I thought you'd take over the shop,' she'd said instead.

'What difference could it make to wait, Francis?'

'There's nothing to wait for.'

As long as he lived Francis knew he would never forgive himself. As long as he lived he would say to himself that he hadn't been able to wait a few years, until she'd passed quietly on. He might even have been in the room with her when it happened.

'It was a terrible thing not to tell me,' he said. 'I sat down and wrote her a postcard, Paul. I bought her a plate.'

'So you said.'

'You're drinking too much of that whisky.'

'Now, Francis, don't be silly.'

'You're half drunk and she's lying there.'

'She can't be brought back no matter what we do.'

'She never hurt anyone,' Francis said.

Father Paul didn't deny that, although it wasn't true. She had hurt their sister Kitty, constantly reproaching her for marrying the man she had, long after Kitty was aware she'd made a mistake. She'd driven Edna to Canada after Edna, still unmarried, had had a miscarriage that only the family knew about. She had made a shadow out of Francis although Francis didn't know it. Failing to hold on to her other children, she had grasped her youngest to her, as if she had borne him to destroy him.

'It'll be you who'll say a Mass for her?' Francis said.

'Yes, of course it will.'

'You should have told me.'

Francis realized why, all day, he'd been disappointed. From the moment when the hired car had pulled into the lay-by and his brother had pointed across the valley at the Garden of Gethsemane he'd been disappointed and had not admitted it. He'd been disappointed in the Via Dolorosa and in the Church of the Holy Sepulchre and in Bethlehem. He remembered the bespectacled man who'd kept saying that you couldn't be sure about anything. All the people with cameras made it impossible to think, all the jostling and pushing was distracting. When he'd said there'd been too much to take in he'd meant something different.

'Her death got in the way,' he said.

'What d'you mean, Francis?'

'It didn't feel like Jerusalem, it didn't feel like Bethlehem.'

'But it is, Francis, it is.'

'There are soldiers with guns all over the place. And a girl came up to me on the street. There was that man with a bit of the Cross. There's you, drinking and smoking in this place – '

'Now, listen to me, Francis – '

'Nazareth would be a disappointment. And the Sea of Galilee. And the Church of the Loaves and Fishes.' His voice had risen. He lowered it again. 'I couldn't believe in the Stations this morning. I couldn't see it happening the way I do at home.'

'That's nothing to do with her death, Francis. You've got a bit of jet-lag, you'll settle yourself up in Galilee. There's an atmosphere in Galilee that nobody misses.'

'I'm not going near Galilee.' He struck the surface of the table, and Father Paul told him to contain himself. People turned their heads, aware that anger had erupted in the pale-faced man with the priest.

'Quieten up,' Father Paul commanded sharply, but Francis didn't.

'She knew I'd be better at home,' he shouted, his voice shrill and reedy. 'She knew I was making a fool of myself, a man out of a shop trying to be big – '

'Will you keep your voice down? Of course you're not making a fool of yourself.'

'Will you find out about planes tomorrow morning?'

Father Paul sat for a moment longer, not saying anything, hoping his brother would say he was sorry. Naturally it was a shock, naturally he'd be emotional and feel guilty, in a moment it would be better. But it wasn't, and Francis didn't say he was sorry. Instead he began to weep.

'Let's go up to your room,' Father Paul said, 'and I'll fix about the plane.'

Francis nodded but did not move. His sobbing ceased, and then he said, 'I'll always hate the Holy Land now.'

'No need for that, Francis.'

But Francis felt there was and he felt he would hate, as well, the brother he had admired for as long as he could remember. In the lounge of the Plaza Hotel he felt mockery surfacing everywhere. His brother's deceit, and the endless whisky in his brother's glass, and his casualness after a death seemed like the scorning of a Church which honoured so steadfastly the mother of its founder. Vivid in his mind, his own mother's eyes reminded him that they'd told him he was making a mistake, and upbraided him for not heeding her. Of course there was mockery everywhere, in the splinter of wood beneath plastic, and in the soldiers with guns that were not toys, and the writhing nakedness in the Holy City. He'd become part of it himself, sending postcards to the dead. Not speaking again to his brother, he went to his room to pray.

'Eight a.m., sir,' the girl at the reception desk said, and Father Paul asked that arrangements should be made to book two seats on the plane, explaining that it was an emergency, that a death had occurred. 'It will be all right, sir,' the girl promised.

He went slowly downstairs to the bar. He sat in a corner and lit a cigarette and ordered two whiskies and ice, as if expecting a companion. He drank them both himself and ordered more. Francis would return to Co. Tipperary and after the funeral he would take up again the life she had ordained for him. In his brown cotton coat he would serve customers with nails and hinges and wire. He would regularly go to Mass and to Confession and to Men's Confraternity. He would sit alone in the lace-curtained sitting-room, lonely for the woman who had made him what he was, married forever to her memory.

Father Paul lit a fresh cigarette from the butt of the last one. He continued to order whisky in two glasses. Already he could sense the hatred that Francis had earlier felt taking root in himself. He

wondered if he would ever again return in July to
Co. Tipperary, and imagined he would not.

At midnight he rose to make the journey to bed
and found himself unsteady on his feet. People
looked at him, thinking it disgraceful for a priest to
be drunk in Jerusalem, with cigarette ash all over his
clerical clothes.